THE TORN BIBLE

Or

Hubert's Best Friend

By

ALICE SOMERTON

www.trafford.com

© Copyright 2003 Revised edition by Norman P. Flout. All rights reserved.

The 1869, 4th Edition w/illustrations revised, edited, published by Norman P. Flout, Louisville, KY USA in association with Trafford Publishing.

No part of this publication may be reproduced, stored in a retrieval system, or transmitted, in any form or by any means, electronic, mechanical, photocopying, recording, or otherwise, without the written prior permission of the author.

```
National Library of Canada Cataloguing in Publication Data

Somerton, Alice
     The Torn Bible / Alice Somerton.
ISBN 1-55395-781-4
     I. Title.
PR6119.O44T67 2003                              823'.92
C2003-900742-1
```

TRAFFORD

This book was published *on-demand* in cooperation with Trafford Publishing.
On-demand publishing is a unique process and service of making a book available for retail sale to the public taking advantage of on-demand manufacturing and Internet marketing. **On-demand publishing** includes promotions, retail sales, manufacturing, order fulfilment, accounting and collecting royalties on behalf of the author.

Suite 6E, 2333 Government St., Victoria, B.C. V8T 4P4, CANADA
Phone   250-383-6864   Toll-free   1-888-232-4444 (Canada & US)
Fax   250-383-6804   E-mail   sales@trafford.com
Web site   www.trafford.com   TRAFFORD PUBLISHING IS A DIVISION OF TRAFFORD HOLDINGS LTD.
Trafford Catalogue #03-0144   www.trafford.com/robots/03-0144.html

10   9   8   7   6   5   4   3   2

TO GLANVILLE and HIS EIGHT SCHOOL FELLOWS

Perhaps, dear boys, you wonder why I should have dedicated this little book to you: It is that you may feel a deeper interest in it, and imbibe, from reading it an earnest love and reverence for your Bible, which, like a good angel, can guide you safely through the world as long as you live. Like Hubert's mother, I ask you to read a portion every day, and whatever be the battle of life you may have to fight, may God's blessing attend you, making you more humble towards Him, dutiful to your parents, and a blessing to mankind.

Believe me,

Yours affectionately,

ALICE SOMERTON

About This Book and Its Author

This Revised Edition is based on the 1869, 4th edition with illustrations.

Special thanks go to my wife Deborah for her time given in typing and reviewing of this book. She has demonstrated much patience with me throughout this whole project.

From the author's account, the Goodwin family was "well to do in the world, and descended from a family of some distinction." The Goodwins lived in Hulney, a tiny village in the north of England, north of Alnwick. By historical account, this tiny village saw Margaret, wife of Henry VI take refuge in its ancient church as well as one hundred of the heroes of Flodden Field rest there on their return from victory.

At the time of this printing, my latest research has determined that Hulney is actually Hulne Priory, and information on Alice Somerton is presently non-existent.

Hannah Lowe found this book while living in the New York metropolitan area and rescued it to a new life of use. One of the founding members of The New Testament Missionary Fellowship, Hannah Lowe (she and her husband Thomas were missionaries to the nation of Columbia from 1934 to 1980) had a penchant for finding old books in used bookstores and purchasing them so that they could be placed in the library of the house church.

My first contact with this story came in the early nineties while living in the house church of the New Testament Missionary

Fellowship, located in Yonkers, New York. Looking for something to read one evening, I began perusing the library shelves for a thought-provoking book; I stumbled across this most excellent read. Had I known that God would lead me on a quest to publish this book and get it into the hands of as many people as possible, I probably would not have even picked it up. But, as many of us know, God's ways are not our ways, and He is patient in waiting for His will to come to pass.

Now, almost nine years since I first picked up this book to read, it is once again available as an encouragement to parents as they struggle to raise their children in these most often difficult times. I pray that the message contained within this story will enlighten your hearts and minds and encourage you to pray, and never give up on your children, no matter how difficult things may seem.

Be blessed and encouraged!

Norman P. Flout

Contents

I	HUBERT'S DEPARTURE FROM HOME	1
II	TOO LATE FOR THE POST-BAG	9
III	THE BIBLE TORN	19
IV	ELLEN BUCHAN	31
V	HUBERT WOUNDED	39
VI	THE TIME FOR REFLECTION	45
VII	WHAT THE TORN BIBLE HAD DONE FOR HUBERT	57
VIII	HOMEWARD BOUND	69
IX	TRUE FRIENDSHIP	79
X	THE WANDERER'S RETURN	89
XI	HOME AT LAST	95
XII	MEMORIES OF CHILDISH DAYS	109
XIII	AT REST	117
	APPENDIX	125

THE
TORN BIBLE

CHAPTER I

HUBERT'S DEPARTURE FROM HOME

May thy goodness share with thy birthright!
What heaven more will that these may furnish and my prayers pluck down,
fall on thy head!
Farewell. - SHAKESPEARE

The rural and picturesque village of Hulney, in the north of England is a charming place, it is almost surrounded with well-wooded hills, and the little rivulets, which ever murmur down their sides, run into the limpid stream along the banks of which most of the cottages are built.

At the north end of the village, on the slope of a hill is the church, so thickly covered with ivy that the only portions of the stonework visible are part of the ancient tower and the chancel window.

Legend and historic fact hang their mantle round this old church. History tells us that the brave, yet often cruel, Margaret, wife of

Hubert's Departure from Home

Henry VI, fled there after a defeat in one of her battles, and it is also recorded that one hundred of the heroes of Flodden Field rested there on their return from the victory. Modern times have added to the interest, which clings to this old place, and one thing especially which draws attention will form the subject of this story.

In that old churchyard, where the children of many generations lie side by side, there is many a touching or interesting record, but the stranger ever lingers the longest near seven white gravestones, all bearing the name of Goodwin. Upon the one which has the most recent date is the following inscription: "Sacred to the Memory of Hubert Goodwin, aged seventy years," and below this, a book, partly destroyed, with several of the loose leaves is carved upon the stone, and though perhaps this description of it may not be striking, the exquisite carving of that destroyed book is such that people ask its meaning, and they are told that it is a "torn Bible."

Hubert Goodwin, the tenant of that grave, was the eldest of six children, blessed with pious and affectionate parents, well to do in the world, and descended from a family of some distinction.

Great pains were bestowed upon Hubert's education as he grew up to youth, but from his birth he was of such a passionate turn, and at times so ungovernable, that he was the source of all the sorrow that for many years fell to the lot of his parents; he was different to their other children, and many a time when reproof had been necessary, and the little wayward one, after a troubled day, had retired to rest, his mother's heart, still heavy, led her softly to the bed where he lay sleeping, and there, kneeling down, she would commend him again, with perhaps a deeper earnestness, to that One who knew all her trouble, and whom she

Hubert's Departure from Home

knew could alone help her. Once the boy awoke as his mother knelt beside him, and, as though in answer to her prayer that his heart might be changed, he burst into tears, and throwing his arms round her neck, expressed deep sorrow at having grieved her, and promised to try and do better. Poor mother! Her joy was brief; in a very short time he was as undutiful and rebellious as ever, and so he continued until he reached the age of twelve years, when, as he had determined upon being a soldier, his parents, much against their wish, sent him to a military school, to be educated for the army.

A year rolled away, and all the accounts that came from the master of Hubert's school informed his parents that he was a bold, unruly boy - a great deal of trouble to his teachers - but he would probably tame down a little in time and do very well for the profession he had chosen. Many and many a time these parents wept over the letters which spoke thus of their son: they wished him to be a good soldier - one fearing and serving God - and they oftentimes repeated their tale of sorrow to their good pastor, in whom they were wont to confide, but his mead of comfort was ever the same. What other could he offer? Good man, he knelt with them, directed them to the source of true comfort, the Lord Jesus Christ, and tried to lighten their hearts' burden, by drawing them nearer to the hand that afflicted them.

When Hubert had been three years at school, he obtained, through the influence of friends, a cadetship in one of the regiments belonging to the East India Company, he was still only a boy, and his parents had rather he had not gone entirely away from them so soon, for they felt, and with some truth, that while he was at school he was at least under their protection, if not their guidance. Hubert, however, came home to them a fine noble-looking youth, delighted at the prospect before him, and as

Hubert's Departure from Home

proud and vain as possible at being at last really a soldier. How much his parents loved him, and how they tried to persuade themselves that the vivacity and recklessness he showed arose more from the hilarity of a heart buoyant with youthful spirits, than from an evil nature! But, when on the first Sabbath after his return home, he scoffed at the manner in which they observed that holy day, another arrow pierced their bosoms; another bitter drop fell into their cup of sorrow.

During the three years Hubert had been at school, his parents had gradually observed that, though he did perhaps attend to most of their wishes, there was a careless sort of indifference about him, and though they were always glad to see him in his vacations, they were as glad to see him go back to school, because their home was more peaceful, and everyone was happier when he was not there. Think of this, boys, whoever you may be that are reading this story, and when you spend a short time with those kind parents who love you so much, let them see, by your kindness and willing obedience, that you wish to love them as much as they love you, and never let them have to say that their home is happier when you are not there: no, rather let them rejoice at your coming home, welcome you, and think of you as the bright light that cheers every one in their dwelling, and if they can do that, be assured that God will bless you.

Only a fortnight's leave of absence had been granted to Hubert, and one week had gone. The way in which he had spoken of sacred things, and of the manner in which they had observed the Sabbath, roused his mother, and though her reproof was gentle, she was earnest, and tried all she could to influence him to better thoughts. She told him of the many snares and dangers he would have to encounter, and the many temptations that ever lurk along the path of youth; of the strange country to which he was going, and of the doubly incurred danger of going forth in his own strength. He listened as she talked to him, but along that way which she so dreaded, all his hope and young imagination were centered, and he grew restless and impatient to be gone.

They were busy in Hubert's home; brothers and sisters all helped to forward the things necessary for their elder brother's future comfort, and they sat later than usual round the fire the last night of his stay with them for everything was ready, and the mail-coach would take him from them early on the morrow. The ship which was to convey Hubert to India was to sail from Portsmouth, and as his father was in ill-health, there was some concern in the family circle about his having to take the journey alone; he promised, however, to write immediately when he reached the vessel, and so, with many a kiss and many a prayer, the family separated for the night.

It was a lovely autumn morning, in the year 1792; everything round Hubert's home looked beautiful, and his brothers and sisters, as they clustered around him and gave him their last kisses, each extorted a promise that he would write a long letter to them very soon. Excitement had driven off every regret at parting with him, and one young brother ran off long before the time, to keep watch at the gate for the coach coming.

The time for Hubert to go drew near, and his father, infirm from recent sickness, took his hand as he bade him farewell, and laying the other upon his head, reminded him once more of lessons long ago taught, and long ago forgotten; gave him again good counsel concerning his future life; then pressed him earnestly to his heart, and prayed God to keep him. Then came his mother; she had already poured out the deep sorrow she felt at his leaving her, and had endeavored to school herself to the parting; without

Hubert's Departure from Home

a word she threw her arms round his neck and bent her head for some minutes over him. "Oh, Hubert," she at length said, "when sickness or trouble comes upon you, you will be far from home, and there will be none of us who love you so dearly near to comfort you, and no one to try and guide you right, but see here, I have a Bible; take it, treasure it as my last gift, and promise me that you will read it every day. I care not how little you read, but promise that you will read some, you will never regret it, and may it teach you the way to heaven."

"I *will* read it, mother; I wish I were as good as you are; I know I am not like the others. Mother dear, don't cry: I will try and do as you wish: good-bye!" and after kissing her affectionately, he hurried from the house.

The coach was at the gate, round which the children gathered, and for a few minutes everyone seemed busy. The servant-man was there with Hubert's trunk and a small leather bag; the nurse had come round from the back garden with the baby; cook followed, and stood a little way behind the gate with her arms half wrapped up in her apron, and the housemaid stood at one of the open bedroom windows while on the steps of the door were his parents, joining in the farewell to the firstborn. Pilot, the house dog, seemed to have some notion of the passing event, for he had come to the gate too, and did not, as was his usual custom, race and gambol with the children, but sat down amongst them all, apparently in a thoughtful mood. Hubert kissed his brothers and sisters, and then took his seat amongst the passengers; then came many a good-bye, and waving of handkerchiefs, and the coach rolled away.

Hubert's Departure from Home

Hubert's Departure

Hubert's Departure from Home

"He's gone," said his father, as the coach wended its way round the hill; "never mind, Mary; it was not for this we trained him, but we've done our duty, I hope, in letting him go, for he was determined, and would perhaps soon have taken his own way, poor lad! Perhaps amongst strangers he will do better than with us, but I would sooner have buried him-sooner, by far, have laid him in the churchyard-than he should have taken this course. What is the use of trying to make children good? Tears, prayers, self-denials, what is the use of them all if the result is like this?" So he murmured, and then bowed his head and wept, and his wife, instead of receiving comfort from him, became the comforter for, putting her arm round his neck, she replied, "oh, yes, dear, our prayers and tears have brought us many blessings; see the other children, how good they are; don't murmur. God may yet bless us in Hubert; it is terrible to part with him in this way but it may yet be a blessing to us all, God knows." Then she sat down and wept with her husband over this first great sorrow, and they *did* weep, they and God alone knew the depth of the woe that had come upon them; the first-born pride of their home and hearts, going from them, perhaps for ever, without one religious impression, or care for the future was a sorrow that none around could lighten, and they knelt down and prayed fervently for that reckless son, and tried to feel a deeper trust in Him, who, though depriving them of one blessing, gave them many.

CHAPTER II

TOO LATE FOR THE POST-BAG

Be wise today; 'tis madness to defer; next day the fatal precedent will plead; thus on, till wisdom is pushed out of life. - YOUNG

Meantime, Hubert went on his way, and a feeling of sadness came over him after he lost sight of his home amongst the trees; for the thought had come into his mind, that perhaps he might never see it again. For a moment his heart beat quickly, and he gave a deep sigh; then, putting his hand into the leather bag, he was just going to take out his mother's present to him, when a man, who sat opposite, said, "I suppose, young soldier, you are off to join your regiment?"

"Yes," replied Hubert with a smile, and as he drew his hand from the bag, he continued, "we are ordered to the East Indies."

"East Indies eh, you'll soon see a little life, they tell me there's plenty of fighting going on out yonder, though we don't get much of it in the newspaper, but you are very young!"

"Yes, I'm the youngest cadet in the regiment; I'm just turned fifteen, but I shall be as brave as my any of the others, I dare say, and I mean to make as good a soldier."

"No doubt of it," replied more than one of the passengers, and the coachman, who had heard the conversation, cracked his whip, as he chimed in, "Hear! Hear! Well done!" Then, as the coach rolled along over many a mile, they talked of nothing but Hubert, and the sphere of his future existence. It feasted the boy's pride, and every other thought fled away, and he forgot all about his home and his Bible.

It was the morning of the third day since Hubert started, when, after many changes and delays, the journey was almost ended, and in less than an hour they would be in London.

"Do you go to your ship at once?" inquired a gentleman who was seated beside the coachman, and whom had not only come all the journey with Hubert, but also who appeared particularly interested in him.

"I should like to go very much," replied the boy, "because I know no one in London, though my leave of absence is not up till tomorrow."

"My brother is captain of your vessel," said the stranger, "so, if you like, we can go together, for I am on the way to say good-bye to him."

Nothing could have suited Hubert better; so, upon leaving the coach, which reached London as the clocks were striking five, they hurried off to the street where the mail started for Portsmouth, and after traveling all day they reached the vessel. How happy was Hubert that night! What a joyous glow was on his cheek! Several of his old companions were there, and not one of them appeared to have any sorrow at leaving friends and home; they greeted each other with light hearts and buoyant spirits, talked of the varied enjoyments of the past holiday, and laughed loud and long as they sat together in the mess room.

Too Late for the Post-Bag

Here and there, apart from the young ones, in nook and corner, or leaning over the side of the vessel and older head resting upon the hand, told that, with some, at least, the pang of parting from home and dear ones had left its impress upon the heart of the soldier, and there was one young lad, a stranger, only one month older than Hubert, seated upon a coil of rope weeping as though his heart would break. The little cabin boy, a child of eleven, tried to soothe him, but the sailors, as they passed by, said, "Let him alone, boy, and he'll join his mess mates below all the sooner."

Night closed at last, and for a few hours, at least, there was silence: sleep may not have visited every pillow, but the loud laugh was hushed, and the stillness of night rested upon the vessel.

It was late the next morning when Hubert left his cabin; all was noise and confusion; hundreds of soldiers were moving about, and Hubert, to escape from the turmoil, was preparing to go ashore, when a superior officer touched him on the shoulder and desired him to remain in the vessel. Hubert was vexed at the order, and sat down gloomily upon a seat; the time, however, passed quickly by, and at noon, when the bugle sounded to summon all visitors on deck that they might be sent on shore, he had forgotten his anger, and was one of the most cheerful there.

The friends were gone, all the partings were over, the gangways were secured, and everything was ready. Wind and tide in favor, time was precious, and the roll was called: every soldier, to a man, answered to his name, and they gave three hearty cheers for King George, their regiment, and Old England.

Too Late for the Post-Bag

"The ship will weigh anchor in less than an hour," said a voice close to Hubert's ear, and, turning round, he saw the gentleman who had accompanied him from his home.

"Oh, how do you do?" said Hubert, shaking hands with him. "Do you sail with us?"

"No, only just a mile or so, then I shall return in a boat. Have you a letter to your parents, if so, I shall be happy to post it for you?"

Hubert's face turned red: he had forgotten to write, and he replied, "I have not a letter."

"Perhaps you have already sent one?"

"Yes," said Hubert; "I mean no, I have not written, the ship sails so soon, and I have been so engaged that I forgot."

"Forgot?" said the stranger, retaining his hand. "What, forget to write to those parents you may never see again! Come my lad, that looks ill in a soldier, take a friend's advice, and write a letter at once; if I cannot take it, you will have an opportunity of sending it before many days pass, and your parents must be anxious about you: try and remember all the good counsels they gave you before you left, and never forget them. Good-bye, remember what I say; good-bye."

There was much warmth in the stranger's manner as he shook Hubert's hand, into whose young heart every good resolution returned, and he hastened to the cabin, which he was to share with three other cadets. He was silent and thoughtful as he unpacked his chest to find his writing materials, and there the

Too Late for the Post-Bag

previous evening he had placed his Bible. As he raised the lid, his eye fell upon his mother's last gift, and more earnestly than before he determined upon writing a long letter. The paper was found, and the writing-desk, which a dear little sister had given him, was opened, when in rushed the three noisy companions of his cabin, and made so much disturbance that he found it impossible to write; so, thinking that he should have plenty of time "tomorrow," he put his things back again into his chest, and became as noisy as the others. Another opportunity was lost, another good resolution broken for the society of noisy and riotous companions, and it may be, that the many evils and sorrows of his after-life were but the fruits of his neglecting this first great duty. Had he remembered his parents and their counsels, and cherished the little germ of goodness that was springing up in his heart, heavenly dews might have descended upon the flower, and kept him from the ways of evil.

The vessel at last set sail, and order was restored. Hubert was upon deck, and as he looked over the side of the ship, and saw the white cliffs of his country fading from his view, he for once felt lonely - felt he was leaving all he loved, and he wished he had written home.

"Just a line: I might do it now," he said to himself. He found, however, upon turning to go below, that he would be required to perform one of his military duties almost immediately, so that he could not write then and he felt such a mixture of sorrow and vexation, that the feelings of the boy mocked, as it were, the dress he wore, and leaning his head over the side of the ship, more than one large tear mingled with the waters of the deep.

Their first night at sea came on: how calm and beautiful it was! There was scarcely a ripple upon the ocean; the bright stars in the

Too Late for the Post-Bag

high vault of heaven looked down like so many gentle friends upon the eyes that gazed up at them, and the pale moonbeams lighted up the pathway for those wanderers on the waters. Hubert was not happy: many, many times he fancied he could hear his mother speaking to him, and he would have given much if he had only written to her. It was then he again remembered his Bible, and the promise to read it, which promise he now determined to perform, and as soon as he could conveniently go to his cabin, he did so, opened his chest, and took out the book, intending to read.

"How small it is," he thought, "and how pretty!" Then he turned over leaf by leaf; he knew not where to begin: he could remember nothing at all about it, and it ended in his putting it back in his chest, and going to his bed. Sleep soon silenced every thought, no letter was written home, not a word of the Bible was read, promise and resolutions had passed away with his sorrow, and Hubert little thought, as he silenced the monitor within, how hard it would be to return to the duty he was neglecting. The ship had now been a fortnight at sea; it had passed through the Bay of Biscay, and was off the coast of Portugal, when the soldiers were informed that in about an hour a vessel would pass very near to them and as the sea was calm, a boat would leave in forty minutes to carry letters for England to the passing ship.

"Forty minutes," said Hubert aloud, and apparently pleased, he hurried off, and as many more did, to avail themselves of the opportunity of writing home. Forty minutes, however, was too long a time for Hubert, and he returned again to the deck, to seek a companion and inquire what he intended to do before he himself sat down to write. Thoughts of neglected duty and unkindness to his parents had frequently disturbed Hubert's mind; try as he would to sweep every remembrance of his

Too Late for the Post-Bag

disobedience away, the thought would come that he had not done right, but instead of sorrowing and making an effort to repay the ill he had done, he tried to persuade himself that he was cowardly in giving way to his feelings; so he endeavored to smother the rising affection that stole upon him during the first few days he was upon the sea, and the result was that he became more reckless than ever.

"Letters ready?" All at once startled Hubert, as he stood talking to his companion upon the deck, there was the man with the bag collecting them, and his was not written. The bag was sealed, the boat was pushed off, the last chance, probably for months, was gone, and as he began to hum a tune, he walked away to the other end of the ship. He looked over the side, and momentary feeling of vexation came over him as he saw the little boat carrying its treasure, its bag of home letters, but he was learning now to defy his conscience, and sang louder the snatch of song that rushed to his aid, and seemed to be all he wanted to throw back the better feelings of his heart.

Many weeks had passed since that noble vessel left England; its white sails were still spread in the breeze, and it was wafted on over the sea. Hubert had tried very hard to forget all about his home; the recollections of it were not pleasant, they were too accusing for him to indulge in; there was a holiness about it which ill accorded with the life he was leading, and the effort he continually made to suppress every thought of it frequently caused him to fall deeper into sin.

One night, when in the height of glee in the mess room, when songs were being sung, and the giddy laugh rung out upon the silent waters, and Hubert was joining fully in the mirth of his comrades, he suddenly remembered that he had in his chest a

Too Late for the Post-Bag

book of sea-songs, and hastened away to get it. He knew pretty well where to put his hand upon it; so, when he reached his cabin, he never thought of lighting his little lamp, but knelt down beside his chest in the dark. It was scarcely the work of a minute; his chest was locked, and he skipped away back to the mess room; his hand was upon the door, when all at once his eye fell upon the book he had brought; it was not the one he had intended to bring - it was not the songbook, but the Bible. He started when he saw what he had, and how was it that a sudden chill sped like lightning over him? How was it that on that sultry night he felt so cold? His hand trembled, his heart beat quickly, but the tempter was by his side, and he gave utterance to many an evil thought as he turned back to change that unwelcome treasure.

The Bible was exchanged for the songbook, and Hubert was again with his comrades, where he became more riotous than before, and was nearly the last to retire to rest.

There was silence once more in the ship, for it was midnight, and all except the few who kept the night watch were sleeping. Hubert had perhaps fallen asleep as soon as any of his companions, but his rest was short, for he started up in alarm. He tried to remember what it was that had disturbed him, but could not. He looked around to see if either of his comrades was moving, but their deep, heavy breathing told him they slept, and then he lay down again in his own berth. There, in that still hour, as he listened to the soft wind passing through the rigging, and the slow measured tread of the sentinels on deck, he all at once thought of his English home, thought of his broken faith with his mother, thought of his Bible.

Too Late for the Post-Bag

"It is no use," he said aloud, "I cannot alter it now; how I wish I had but just written home, fool that I was not to do so, and that book, how I wish she had never given it to me; it will make me a coward, in fact it does; I never go to my chest, but there it is; I'll burn it - I'll throw it away; how I wish I had never had it!" and he struck the side of his berth with his clenched fist as he spoke.

There was no voice in that little cabin to answer or direct Hubert in his outburst of passionate feeling and as he looked round at his sleeping comrades, he crept softly from his berth and went and knelt down by his chest. The moon shone brightly through the tiny cabin window, and as he knelt by his chest he could see very well everything around him. He took out his Bible, and gazed wildly at it for a moment, scarce knowing what next to do; then rising as if a sudden thought had struck him, he tried to open the window that he might throw it into the sea: it was, however, too secure to open at his will and turning away after a fruitless effort, he sought a place to hide it. "Where shall I hide it?" he said, as he walked round and round his cabin; there was no nook or corner into which he could thrust it so that it should never meet his eye again. What could he do with it? He must wait for another opportunity; so, taking out nearly everything in his chest, he thrust it down into the farthest corner, heaped all his things upon it, made them secure, and then returned to his bed. The excitement of the moment was over, yet Hubert could not rest and as he turned himself upon his uneasy bed, he never once regretted the wicked thought that had led him to try and throw away his Bible but the determination to dispose of it grew stronger.

Some weeks after this little event, the regiment arrived in India, and was ordered far up the country; the long, toilsome march which Hubert now had to undergo, initiated him into some of the

Too Late for the Post-Bag

realities of a soldier's life, and it was not long before he found that the career he had chosen was not so full of enjoyment as he had anticipated. He very often felt weary; the heat of the country depressed his spirits, and he often sighed deeply as he remembered the pleasant hills and valleys of his own land. The regiment had no sooner located itself in the new station, before Hubert and many others were struck down with fever. Death was busy amongst them, but the young prodigal was spared; many a time he had wished to die; sick and amongst strangers, his mother's words had come home to him with double power, and he felt the bitter truth that there was indeed none who loved him, none to comfort him; it was a wonder he lived, for the fever was malignant, and the care bestowed upon the sick very little indeed. Poor Hubert, how was it he could not die? Young as he was, this illness taught him the sad lesson that, where there is no love or interest, there is an inhumanity in man, and as he grew better, his heart became more hardened, for he began to cherish a hatred towards everyone around him.

CHAPTER III

THE BIBLE TORN

Within this awful volume lies the mystery of mysteries, and better he had ne'er been born who reads to doubt or reads to scorn. - SCOTT

We must pass over a few years. Hubert had overcome the effects of the climate and the many dangers to which he had been exposed, helped, as they ever will, the heart, uninfluenced by religion, to make him more reckless and daring. Away from his sight, at the bottom of his chest, undisturbed, lay his Bible; beside it, too, lay his sister's desk and the writing materials his mother had carefully packed for him; he seldom thought of the fond ones who had given him those things, but far away in England they ever thought of him, and watched and wept for a letter.

Hubert's regiment had seen a great deal of service, and it had not been his lot to escape the dangers of war. On one occasion, he had been overcome and taken prisoner by some natives and was only saved from being put to death in a cruel manner by an unexpected attack being made upon these Hindus by a neighboring chief. The attack left Hubert and two of his companions in the care of some women, from whom they were rescued, by a company of his regiment who had come out to search for him. In a few hours, the attempt to save Hubert would have been in vain, for the Hindus, hating the English, seldom allowed much time to elapse between the capture and the sacrifice. Many a narrow escape besides this, and many a wound - some slight and some severe - dotted the pathway of Hubert's life; the seventh year of his residence in India was drawing to a

The Bible Torn

close. The hot season had been unusually oppressive; nearly every disease which flesh is heir to had made fearful ravages amongst the soldiers, and Hubert was a second time struck down with fever. Mercy once again interposed and like the barren fig tree, he was spared, that another opportunity might be given him to bear fruit. One morning, when he was getting better, the hospital nurse came to him with a letter in her hand, and asked if he thought it was for him; he took it from her, and for a few moments did not answer her: his heart smote him; though his illness had slightly subdued him, he was old in sin, and had learnt how to overcome all feelings of tenderness; so, striving to check the thoughts that were forcing their way, he began to examine the postmarks and various written notices upon the outside of the letter; he soon found how far it had traveled in search of him, and now it was by a mere chance that he had received it.

"Why was this letter not sent after me?" inquired Hubert.

"Be thankful, sir, that you have received it now," said the nurse. "It has traveled after you a great way, but your regiment has been so much on the move, that I am not surprised at its being delayed. I have seen it on the letter-rack more than eight months, and several others with it, and you would not have had it now if I had not remembered you."

"Why, where did you see me before?"

"I nursed poor Captain White in the hospital at Janis and I knew you by your coming so often to see him."

"I did not remember you."

The Bible Torn

"No, sir, perhaps not, but I did you, though it was only this morning that I remembered anything about the letter, and that is how it is they often get delayed: they are given to people very often, to send on, who know nothing at all about them, and so they get put on one side, and sometimes forgotten altogether. I suppose that was sent here because someone knew that when you were stationed here a year ago, you were in hospital with jaundice and here it has been ever since."

"It is high time things were altered, then," replied Hubert, "if this is how the letters are treated."

"Yes, sir, it is," said the nurse, "but you don't seem very anxious to read your letter now you have it."

Hubert said no more. Anxious indeed he was to know what that letter contained, but fearful to open it; the battle; everything indeed in warfare he could face with boldness, but before that silent, soiled, fairy-like packet in his hand his whole nature quailed. Had he been alone, perhaps he would not have opened it at all, but the eye of another was upon him, and perhaps it was to save betrayal that he broke the seal. It was from his father; there was nothing reproachful in it, but a great deal of news about the family, and their affectionate remembrance of him; a long account of letters written, and their fears that they had not reached him; then an earnest pleading that if he received that he would write to them immediately, for their anxiety and disappointment were very great.

Hubert read his letter several times; it was not the first he had received, though perhaps it was the first that he really felt anxious to answer, but he was too much out of health to reply to it then. It was frequently a silent companion to him during the remainder

The Bible Torn

of his stay in the hospital, though when he grew better and returned again to his old companions, somehow his father's letter was forgotten.

Hubert's illness had no effect upon him for good; it was sent, no doubt in mercy, to check, at least for a time, the career he was running, but health had returned, and so had he to his evil habits. Not one thought did he ever willingly give to his parents, or the good precepts they had tried to teach him, but when at times a few lines of a hymn, or a few words of an early learnt prayer, would, in spite of all his efforts, come across his mind, he had become so bold in sin, that he cursed the intruding memory of his purer days.

How little that young soldier thought of the merciful providence that was watching over him! And it was doubtless in answer to his parents' prayers that the little snatches of his early lessons were allowed to intrude so repeatedly upon him, to bring him back, if possible, to a better life. Take courage, mothers, even though the seed now sown seems to perish as it falls, and continue to store up in the little mind passages of holy writ, the simple prayer, and the childish hymn; long, long may the soil remain barren, but a distant storm-cloud may shed its torrents there, and then the fruit of thy labors may return like the autumn grain, and ye shall reap, if ye faint not.

Hubert had grown very handsome, military fortune had smiled upon him, and he had risen to be first lieutenant of his regiment. Good abilities, and great intelligence, with his merry, cheerful disposition, had won him many favors, but those qualities were at the same time the snares in his path: they were misapplied and misdirected, and too often were the cause of his deepest errors.

The Bible Torn

One night, about nine years after Hubert had left England, he sat alone in his room, with a heavier heart than he had ever before endured. His sword lay upon the floor, part of his soldier's dress was thrown carelessly upon a chair, a glass jug of water and a bottle were upon the table, a loose gray cloak was wrapped around him, and his arm was in a sling; he had been in battle that day, and severely cut upon the shoulder, the doctor had attended to him, and bound up the wound, and Hubert, sick and dispirited, lounged in his easy-chair in gloomy silence. The doctor had tried to persuade him to go to bed, and Hubert had promised to do so, but as soon as he was gone, the servant-man was dismissed from the room, and Hubert began to think. They must have been terrible thoughts that could have produced such a look of despair; they were not, however, about his wounded shoulder, nor the dangers he had that day encountered; neither were they of his parents, to whom, in a few months, the news of the battle would probably find its way. It was altogether another matter, which troubled him.

A companion, a fellow officer - the little lad who seated himself upon the coil of rope and wept such tears as the vessel left England - had grown up to manhood with Hubert, and had that morning gone out with him to battle; they were full of spirit when they went, and for some time fought nearly side by side, but there came unexpectedly a terrible volley of shot from a portion of the enemy that lay concealed behind some dense brushwood. Hubert's ranks were thinned and as he turned round to rally and command his men, he missed his friend. It was a critical moment; every energy and thought was required for the fight so that a glance behind, and a fleeting pang lest he had fallen, were all that circumstances allowed, and Hubert rushed on.

The Bible Torn

The battle was won, the soldiers were returning, and Hubert was wounded; he had made inquiry for his friend, but could hear nothing. As they wound their way along, however, by the hillside where the volley had been fired, his heart beat quickly, for his own wound had made him feel weak, and he could scarcely speak, when he saw two soldiers bending over something lying on the grass. All his fears were realized as he slowly came up to the scene, for there, stretched upon the ground, laid his companion, dead. Oh, how the sight overcame him! If man is capable of loving man, it was exemplified in Hubert; for his heart had deeply entwined itself round his hapless comrade, and his first impulse was to kneel beside him, and with his unwounded arm press him to his bosom as he wept over his pallid brow. No thought, however, of the mercy, which had kept him from a similar fate, came into his mind; no prayer of thankfulness went up from his heart, but, sorrowful and ill, he left his friend, and leaning between the two soldiers, he at last, after great difficulty, reached his quarters. After Hubert had been attended to by the doctor, a second thought took the place of the first pure one, and as he sat alone, instead of pouring out his heart in deep gratitude to his Almighty Preserver, he became irritated and angry, and amongst the many thoughts that crowded upon him, he remembered that his poor dead companion was deeply in his debt. Much of their time had been spent together at the gaming-table and only a few evenings before, Hubert had lent his companion all the money he had by him, including his last month's pay; since then, Hubert had gambled and been unsuccessful, and had become involved for a considerable amount, which he had promised to pay in a week, but his companion who owed him sufficient to pay the debt, was killed, and the difficulty into which he was suddenly plunged, drove him almost to despair.

The Bible Torn

"What shall I do?" he said, as he passionately struck the table, and then, in the height of his frenzy, he said many bitter, cruel things about his poor guilty companion, who lay dead upon his bed in the adjoining room.

"Oh, what shall I do?" he said again, and for some minutes he sat still, gazing with a vacant stare upon the floor; then, as if moved by a sudden impulse, he slowly rose from his chair, and, going into his bedroom, he knelt down by his chest, intending to get some writing paper that he might reckon up all he owed and see how far his own resources would help him. Perhaps he was too absorbed to think of what he was doing for he took out a small parcel, and then, after replacing the things in his chest, he went and sat down by the table. For some minutes he sat with his face covered with his hands, as though he were in deep thought; then he muttered something and snatching up the parcel, he broke the string that tied it; one sharp pull drew the paper away, when out upon the table fell his Bible. "Fool, to bring that!" he said, and then he dashed it to the other end of the room. In striking the Bible it came open, and as it came in contact with the corner of a chair, two of its leaves were torn out. There was a slight momentary regret in Hubert's heart, when he found what he had done: he hated the book, and could not bear it in his sight, and though he would have been rid of it, he never thought, nor perhaps ever intended destroying it in that way, and he stepped across the room to gather it all up. Much of his passion subsided as he sat down and tried to replace the torn leaves. The days, however, had long since passed when he was accustomed to read his Bible; he was now not only unfamiliar with that sacred book, but all that he once knew appeared to have gone from his memory, and though he turned over and over again one portion after another, to find the part in Ezekiel from which the pages had been torn, it was of no use, he could not replace them; so

The Bible Torn

with a nervous hand, he thrust them into his pocket, and took the torn Bible back to his chest.

This little incident, though it produced no reflection, subdued for a time the excitement under which he was laboring, and though he disregarded the unseen hand that was dealing so mysteriously with him, the first outburst of bad feeling respecting the difficulty into which he had fallen by the death of his gambling companion was over and leaving his room, he walked with gentle step to the one in which his dead comrade lay. The years of folly and sin, which Hubert had passed, had not quite dried up all the fountains of his heart; one of them at least was flowing afresh as he closed the door, and went up to the remains of his dead friend. He raised the sheet which had been spread over the corpse, and breathed the words, "Oh, poor Harris!" as he gazed upon the once joyous face; then, sitting down beside him, he laid his hand upon the cold forehead, and wept as he had not done since his childhood. He had seen death in many forms, and this was not the first time he had lost a companion, but neither tear nor sigh had followed the death of anyone before, but for poor Harris, how he wept! Hubert had loved him well; death, which before had no effect upon him, overwhelmed him now, and it was not until his own wounded arm grew very painful from the effects of touching the cold dead, that he rose to go away. Harris was to be buried early on the morrow, and Hubert felt such a strange bitterness at parting that he could scarcely go, but at last, bending over him, he pressed one long, fervent kiss upon the silent lips, and turned away.

In passing along near the door, his eye caught what he thought to be a piece of folded paper lying near the clothes of his friend; he picked it up, and upon opening it, found it to be a note from poor Harris - a few lines written by him in pencil, as he lay dying

The Bible Torn

upon the field of battle and there was not much upon the paper, but there was enough. Poor Harris, in that brief note, begged the finder to convey the sad story of his death to his mother, and tell her how bitterly he repented having so long forgotten her; that he begged her to forgive him, and earnestly implored the Lord Jesus to have mercy upon him; then came the words - evidently written by a trembling hand - "Comrade, turn and repent, not a moment may be given to you; tell Hubert Goodwin I am dead: he must meet me again."

Hubert had never felt before what he did as he read that note - written as the life-blood wasted, and he the subject of it; how he trembled, bold, daring soldier that he was! It was the voice from the dead, and at first he felt cold - so cold: his teeth chattered, and then a sudden heat rushed over him, and the perspiration trickled down his face; his bosom swelled, his breath grew short; at length, a long, deep groan burst from his overcharged heart, and he went to his own room. Long, very long, silent and alone, Hubert sat in his dreary chamber; there were but few sounds without, and nothing but sighs and groans broke the stillness within; the words on that blood-spotted note touched him deeply; struck many a note of discord in his heart, tore into shreds the cloak of sin and guilt he had worn so long, and exposed to him the part he had taken in dragging his companion, once a pure, noble-hearted, susceptible boy, down deep into the villainies of his own dissipated life, and he was to meet him again - where?

The teaching of his childhood had not been in vain; the bread cast upon the waters had not all perished; conscience whispered the truth, and Hubert knew where he should meet Harris. The soldier's head bowed; he felt he could not, he dare not, meet the soul he had ruined; the thought of the terrible record against him

The Bible Torn

The Bible Torn

The Bible Torn

broke down his spirit. "Great God!" as he glanced upward, was all he uttered in his despair, and his head drooped again in deep anguish upon his bosom.

CHAPTER IV

ELLEN BUCHAN

She was the pride of her familiar sphere, - the daily joy of all whom on her gracefulness might gaze, and in the light and music of her way have a companion's portion. Who could feel, while looking upon beauty such as hers, that it would ever perish? - WILLIS

That night, and for many days, Hubert knew no peace; sleeping or waking, Harris was ever in his thoughts; turn where he would, there was a remembrance of his dead companion, the loss of whom he deeply mourned. Out of health himself, his bereavement was more felt, especially as he was unable to seek other comrades with whom he might drive gloomy thoughts away. At other times, when he had been ill, Harris had ever sought him, but now, no one save those who waited upon him entered his room, and he began to hate the sound of their footsteps, because he felt that he paid for their sympathy. Poor Harris! How he missed him, how long the days seemed, and how slow his recovery! Who shall say it was not an opportunity vouchsafed by the Almighty to bring back his own wandering soul? Why did he not pray in his hours of distress? No, the heart long used to the neglect of the holy privilege and duty, but ill knows how to fly to the throne of grace in the hour of woe, but too often throws back the hand of God with ungrateful murmuring. Hubert never once poured out his burden of distress; never once looked to that loving God whose eye, notwithstanding his wickedness, watched over him with a father's love, but fretted and repined at the calamity which had befallen him, until every pure and good feeling fled away once more, and he began to be as cold and callous about the death of poor Harris as he was about other things.

Time, the great soother of woe in the human heart, threw its power over Hubert; as it passed, it brought him returning health and once again mingling in the busy scenes of his profession, the wounded arm, the dead companion, and the warning, all shared the doom of the other events of his life: they were gone, and he was happy in forgetting them. The difficulty into which he had fallen with respect to his money matters, however, taught him a lesson, and though he again joined the society of many of his former companions, he never again fell into that terrible vice, which had so nearly ruined his worldly prospects.

Some weeks had passed away; all the little effects belonging to poor Harris were being collected, for the captain of his company had found amongst some letters, the names of some of the poor fellow's relations in England. Hubert heard of what was being done, and one morning, meeting the doctor of the regiment, they began talking the matter over. "I can tell you where his mother lives," said Hubert, "if you will step into my rooms; for now I remember it, I have by me a little note for her, at least I have her address upon it."

They walked along together, talking of various matters, and having reached Hubert's rooms, he took from a little desk a small piece of paper and without a thought said, as he handed it to the doctor, "I think you'll find it on that."

The doctor read the note and as he did so, a sad expression stole over his face, and then, looking at Hubert, he said, "Oh, Goodwin, what a letter! Poor Harris! What a warning for us all, and what an escape you had; the ball passed you, but it pierced his lungs; it might have been your lot; though I trust a better account than this would have been sent home of you."

"Come now doctor, no preaching; I cannot tell what account will be given of me when I'm knocked off."

"A true one, I have no doubt," was the reply.

"Perhaps so, but I don't care what people say; I do my duty, no one can deny that, and soldiers can't be preachers."

"But they can be Christians and find as much need of the Bible as the sword. As much, ah more! It is a double weapon, a sword and a shield; try it, Goodwin, if you never have, and see if I am not correct. If any man is in heaven, my father is; he was thirty-four years a soldier, fought in forty-one battles and had as many wounds, and what preserved him? What made him go cheerfully through all the trials of a soldier's life? What made his name honored and respected, as you yourself have often observed? Was it the battles he fought, or the fame he won? No, he read his Bible every day of his life and tried to live as that holy book says men ought to live. He infused, by God's help, the same spirit into his company, and many a year must roll by before the words, "Good Captain Martin,' will cease to be heard and the influence of his example will linger still longer. No one can tell the power of example and it is a serious reflection, that we each have to answer for the amount we exercise over our fellow-creatures."

Hubert had thrown himself into an easy-chair, and with his hands thrust into his pockets, he silently listened to the doctor, but now he replied: "But surely we cannot possibly help persons imitating what we do; I don't see that we are to be responsible for the folly and evil deeds of others."

"Certainly not, Goodwin, but still, how can we be sure that our conduct has not caused many of the deeds you mention? Thousands of noble-hearted, pure-minded youths, who have entered the army have been ruined, both in body and soul, by the example of some wicked comrade."

"Do you refer to Harris?" asked Hubert, starting up from his seat; "because if you do, I may tell you at once that I am not going to be accused of anything he did. If he chose to make a fool of himself, it is nothing to me, my conscience is clear."

"I refer to truth," said the doctor, "and my own experience, and if we would only ask ourselves how far our conduct will affect those around us, we should be better men. Man will imitate, and it is what he imitates that ennobles or debases him; it is example which has filled the heart of man with all that is good and noble, and it has also helped to make up long catalogues of crime. Our blessed Savior knew the power of it when he said to his disciples, 'Be ye perfect, as I am perfect.'"

The calm and gentle manner of the doctor subdued Hubert's rising anger and as he listened to him, he also felt the deep power of example. Before any other man who had dared to refer to Harris as his heart told him the doctor had done, he would have given way to the passion which his guilty conscience prompted, but-there was an overpowering influence in the calm demeanor of that good man, which Hubert felt, and when he was gone the room seemed very lonely, and Hubert paced it with rapid stride, as he thought over the past: the life he had led and was still leading, the dead Harris and the warning note smote upon his memory and he wished, oh how earnestly he wished, that he were but half like that good man who had just left him! It was a difficult matter however for Hubert to profit much by what had transpired; the wish to lead a better life was earnest enough, but old habits and evil associates had forged their chains of fascination round him, and he went out to seek company which would soon snap the silver cord of purity that was beginning once more to form holy tracery on his heart.

Thus it ever is with the heart that is continually striving against the influences and power of the Spirit. To keep down the still small voice of conscience, nothing is so effectual as the whirlwind of pleasure, and man runs headlong from one sin to another, until the fatal hour dawns when God's Spirit will no longer strive. Repeated warnings disregarded, and opportunities neglected, ruined Hubert's better nature: in scenes of dissipation the germs of holiness perished, and he sunk down deep, deeper still into sin, growing older in wickedness as he grew stronger in manhood, belying, as many do, the noble image on his brow, by the mark of *Cain* upon his heart.

It was seldom that the regiment to which Hubert belonged remained longer than a few years in one place, so that his stock of worldly possessions had not greatly increased, but it was eighteen years since he left home, and he was now about changing into another regiment, one more stationary than his own, and marrying the daughter of an old English resident at Agra. During the time Hubert had been in India, he had experienced many vicissitudes, often marching through the country, often in battle and occasionally sick and in hospital. He had grown from the pretty rosy boy to a tall, dark; sun burnt man and was now a captain. In military things he had improved, but though of those who went out with him to India more than half had either fallen in battle or died of disease, nothing softened his heart and it was a wicked boast he frequently made in the mess room, that when he was unable to fight any longer he would think about going home and being religious. Thus he went on wasting the vigor of his life, tempting by his blasphemy the merciful God that was sparing him, neglecting every opportunity for repentance, and occasionally tearing up his Bible.

The doctor, who had been nearly the same time in the regiment that Hubert had, but who in age was ten years his senior, never lost an opportunity of trying to influence the soldiers for good. Many a rebuff was the reward of the good man's efforts, but he never wearied. Hubert, though he listened to him once, had grown vain with his military promotion and shunned the good man who had once brought his heart near to heaven. Dr. Martin, however, never lost sight of the reckless sinner, but breathed many a sigh as he thought of one so gifted, and placed so far above the wants of life, rushing fast to his ruin, and then he prayed, with all the earnestness of a devoted heart, that God's Spirit would stay him in his course of sin.

Like a gleam of light upon a darkened object came the news that Hubert was about to be married to Ellen Buchan. Nearly every one in Agra knew her and there were but few who did not also know how good she was; she and her family were distinguished for their piety, and many a darkened soul in the idolatrous city were they resided learnt by their teaching and example to place Christianity above the idol worship of their childhood and became followers of the meek and lowly Jesus. Surely such companionship as Ellen Buchan would be a blessing to Hubert, and a change must come upon him, else he would be no helpmate for one so good as she was, and the doctor wondered whether a change had not already come over him by his having expressed an intention of moving into another regiment.

Ellen Buchan

How fervently he hoped that it might be so, and though he now seldom exchanged a word with Hubert, he did not forget him, but still hoped that he might lead a better life. Imperceptibly to Hubert, a change had indeed stolen over him since he knew Ellen; many of his old haunts were forsaken, former friends were given up, and Hubert had something to bear from the taunting words and manners of his old associates, but he had other thoughts, new habits were being formed, life had a thousand charms, and his face beamed more joyous and more handsome every day; his chief desire was to sell out, and purchase in the regiment stationed at Agra. A few disappointments attended Hubert's change of regiment: it was delayed longer than he had expected; still, the matter was now, to all appearance, nearly settled and preparations were being made for the marriage. If Hubert had ever been thoroughly happy, he appeared so now: his past life, with all its associations, was absorbed in the present, in Ellen every thought was centered.

Alas! How frail are man's hopes. One sultry evening a messenger came to tell Hubert to come at once to Mr. Buchan's, for something had happened.

With a beating heart and hurried step he hastened to the house, but there was sorrow there. Ellen had been complaining all day and as the evening drew on, her illness increased, and she was found to be suffering from fever. Hubert was frightened, for the fever had been prevalent, and frequently fatal. That night and the next day he stayed at the house and then, how dreadful came the news that her life was despaired of! Now Hubert felt, perhaps for the first time in his life, the bitter woe of hopes all crushed; for the thought of losing Ellen was terrible. What could he do! All around him was a scene of woe. Changed he apparently was in his conduct and habits, but his heart was the same and his sorrow gave way to murmuring and raving about the affliction. How earnestly he hoped for her recovery, yet how unchastened was his spirit! For upon meeting Dr. Martin who, after inquiring about Ellen, added kindly, "I hope, if only for your sake, she will recover," he replied sharply, "Sir, you hope nothing of the kind; if she dies you will upbraid and taunt me." Unjust and cruel as this remark was, the doctor pitied and forgave him and stood gazing after him as he turned away.

Ellen died. We need not tell the deep bereavement it was to all who loved her. Reader, it matters nothing to thee, but there was a home made desolate and more than one heart riven! Such is life! A time will come when the deep mystery of such dealings shall be explained; till then, hope on! Trust on! Believe on! Satan would tempt thee in the weak-trying hour to doubt, but remember, God does not willingly afflict. The finest gold has been seven times purified and happy is he who can look upward, even though it be through his tears and say, "It is thy will, Lord; do with me as it seemeth thee good."

All who knew Hubert pitied him under the deep affliction, which had befallen him, and for a time his spirit bowed beneath it. He overcame it however, sooner than many had expected, joined himself again to many of his old companions and gave up all intention of selling out of his regiment. Very soon he bade farewell to the friends he had made in Agra and moved with his regiment to a station further up the country.

CHAPTER V

HUBERT WOUNDED

On comes the foe - to arms, to arms, we meet - 'tis to death or glory; 'tis victory in all her charms, or fame in Britain's story. - W. SMYTH

Three more years passed away. It had been a trying time, for a native tribe near a neighboring jungle gave Hubert's regiment continual trouble, and now orders were received at the barracks to prepare for a battle, for large numbers of Hindus were coming down from the hills and several British regiments were on the march to assist the station that was menaced.

Hubert received the order and gave it out again to his company and then, without another word, went to his rooms. It was not his usual way, he generally said something in praise of British bravery and tried to inspire his men to action but this time he was silent. The soldiers did not let it pass without remark.

Never before had the order for battle been less welcome. He was unable to account for the strange depression of his spirits; he joined none of his companions, but sat the whole evening by himself and retired to rest much earlier than usual. His sleep, however, was disturbed and once, in the still hour of night, he said aloud, "What ails me that I cannot sleep? I am not ill. I wonder if anything is to happen to me. Surely not, after nearly twenty-two years' service, I am to have better luck than be knocked off now. It is a pretty safe thing, they say, if one gets over the twentieth year. I shall see old England yet." No more sleep, however, came to him; he thought of his home, his parents and all to whom he had been dear and he sighed deeply as he wished he had loved them better.

The morning sun had scarcely risen before the bugle sounded and in a very short time the regiment was on the march, for they had six miles to go and the heat would be against them later in the day.

On the previous evening, Hubert had passed some of the dull hours in looking over the little relics he had collected during his residence in India. In sorting through the box he had brought with him from England, he took out the remains of his Bible. It was sadly destroyed. The covers, some of the Old and the greater part of the New Testament, were what remained of it. After hesitating for a few minutes what he should do with it, he thrust it into a pocket in the left side of the bosom of his coat. It was there still; he had forgotten to remove it when he rose hastily at the sound of the bugle and as he marched with his regiment. He little thought of the blessing, which that torn, despised treasure, would yet be to him. It was a long, toilsome march, through thick jungle and the soldiers sat down to rest when they got through it and waited to be joined by other forces. They had come out against a considerable village, the residence of a great chief, but not so well fortified by architectural defenses, as by the hordes of its savage inhabitants. From the spot where the soldiers rested, they could see the place they had come to attack and as the day was passing without the other regiments appearing, a council was held and beneath the shadow of the palm trees, the soldiers received orders to remain quiet until new commands were issued.

The day at length was closing and Hubert with three brother officers, sat down beneath a tree together. At first they talked of

Hubert Wounded

the glory in fighting for their king and country, then other matters connected with military life followed, but as the time passed away, and the hours of night brought with them their fitful gloom, the conversation changed and for the first time for many years Hubert talked of his home.

"It is a long time since I left England," he said; "many, many a year, and I have somehow neglected all my old friends there. I often wish I had acted differently and thought a little more about them and written to them sometimes, but it is no use regretting. Not that I have much to regret, though, for letter-writing is a silly, dawdling business at best and never was much in my way, but, however, should it so happen tomorrow that the chances run against me - you know what I mean - well, there's some one of the family left, perhaps who will like to know the end of me; so let me ask a favor. Take this slip of paper and if your luck is better than mine, just send a letter to that address and tell them where your old comrade fell and tell them he - nay! tell them what you like."

The three officers each took down Hubert's address and promised to perform his wish, but they too had friends and relations in Britain's distant isle and they each asked of Hubert a similar boon should the fortune of the day be his and not theirs. Then with a friendly grasp of the hand, they exchanged promises, and to think perhaps more deeply of the past, or the morrow, they bade each other goodnight and lay down in silence on the ground. Only for a few hours did anything like stillness hover over the beleaguered village; at early dawn the natives, having heard that the English were surrounding them, came out in great numbers, to drive away or attack their invaders. A terrible fight now commenced, wearing any form but that of a set battle and it lasted the whole day, but at length the chief was slain and the

Hubert Wounded

Hindus, upon hearing it, fled in all directions, leaving the English masters of the village. There had been a sad slaughter of the natives, and more than two hundred of the English had fallen. Hubert's regiment had suffered considerably, but he and his three companions were spared and they met again in the same place where they had passed the previous evening; neither wound nor mark of warfare was upon any of them; they were only fatigued and as they shook each other by the hand, they used some of their old familiar terms of friendship and sat down again beneath the tree. There was no talk of home now, no thought of the gracious shield, which had preserved them in the fight, no word of thanksgiving to Almighty God for their safety.

As night came on, they proceeded to the captured village, but in the morning, as all the soldiers were not required to remain, Hubert's company and one or two others, were ordered back to their respective barracks. Several of Hubert's company was missing; familiar faces were gone and well-remembered voices were hushed. Yet with pride and high spirits, most of those that remained, after having helped to bury some of the dead, prepared to march as soon as the sun would permit. It was a beautiful evening when the soldiers started, but they had not gone very far before Hubert and some of the other officers fell a little behind the men and sat down upon the short, dry grass and weeds. Just as they were about to pursue their journey through the jungle, some beautiful birds attracted their attention and they turned aside from the pathway in pursuit. This thoughtless act was attended with danger, for the evening was fast closing and there was every probability that they would lose their way. At the suggestion of one, however, they turned back and made all possible haste to overtake the soldiers. Night came on much more rapidly than they had expected and before they had gone far in the jungle, it grew very dark. They pushed on as rapidly as they

Hubert Wounded

could, but the path was unfamiliar to them, and they soon lost each other. Sometimes a rustling amongst the bushes made Hubert start, and once he thought he heard voices besides the scattered ones of his companions. Very soon however, all was silent. They were all wandering different ways, and Hubert was alone. Once he thought of climbing into a tree and staying there till daybreak, but he felt so confident that he could not have much further to go, that he made another effort to reach the barracks. Suddenly, a rustling in the bush startled him again and laying his hand upon his sword, he called out the watchword of his regiment. There was no answer. Thinking it perhaps some bird, he went on again, keeping up his courage by occasionally whistling. He had almost reached the edge of the jungle, for he had fortunately kept near the right path, when a wild shout fell upon his ear, a flash of light illumined all around him and Hubert, stunned and wounded, fell to the ground.

The moon rose calmly in the sky and her soft rays fell upon the trees beneath which Hubert lay. He was still insensible and the brown grass around him was stained with blood. A slight breath of wind that passed over him gently waved the dark hair from his wounded forehead; another ball had shattered his right leg, which had bent up beneath him as he fell.

The next morning, not far away, in the barracks, the roll was called. Hubert's companions had arrived safe during the night; they now told where they had missed him and a piquet of men were sent out to search for him. They did not go far into the jungle before Hubert was found. He had partly recovered from his faintness, but was too exhausted to speak; they conveyed him to the hospital, where his wounds were dressed and every attention was paid him, but he had lost so much blood as he lay

Hubert Wounded

all night upon the ground, that no hopes whatever were given of his recovery and he lay several days without speaking a word.

The doctor came day after day, as often as he could snatch a moment from his duties and sat down by Hubert's bed. He knew all about him, knew the life he had led and felt all the weight of the dread thought of a soul passing into eternity unsaved. There he lay, that reckless, sinning one, now helpless, dying and many a heartfelt prayer was breathed by the one friend that still clung to him, that he might not be taken away in his sin. It is not kith nor kin that bounds the Christian's love. Like his Divine Master, he deems precious every human soul and no matter 'neath what sky or color, whether friend or foe, he cannot see that priceless thing perish without an effort to save it. Many long hours the doctor sat and watched by Hubert's bed. The leg had been set and appeared favorable, but reason did not return and it was for that he watched and prayed and yet how that same reason had shunned and insulted him. Good man, he forgot all about himself now, and watched as a fond brother over the sufferer. His prayers were heard: Hubert awoke from insensibility, and occasionally spoke a word to those who attended him.

CHAPTER VI

THE TIME FOR REFLECTION

O, lost and found! All gentle souls below their dearest welcome shall prepare, and prove such joy o'er thee, as raptured seraphs know, who learn their lesson at the throne of love. - KEBLE

A week had passed. Hubert was slightly better and there was a faint hope that he would ultimately recover. The doctor had been two or three times during each day to see him and now, as the sun was setting, he came again. Weary as he was with his usual duties, he had still his Master's work to do and as he took his seat by Hubert's bed, he asked if he should read to him. Hubert knew quite well that the doctor's book was the Bible and though he also knew that very faint hopes were given of his recovery, he replied: "No, thank you; I shall perhaps soon be better, when I shall have plenty of time to read." The doctor tried to prevail, but Hubert resisted, until he became excited, when his friend, wishing him a goodnight, left him alone.

"Yes, I hope soon to be better," he repeated to himself, as the doctor left the room. Though, as he gazed at the three empty beds near him, he little thought that the insensibility to all pain which occasionally stole over him, rendered the hope of his recovery very faint and that, unless a change took place, his couch would soon be empty also.

Another and another day passed. Hubert was no better, and as the doctor again sat down beside him, he said, as he gently took the feverish hand, "My friend, perhaps you would like someone

The Time for Reflection

to send a letter to your friends in England; is there anything you would like to say? Shall I write for you?"

"Not now."

"Why not now? I have told you how precarious your state is. You had better send a few lines home. Let me write something for you; shall I?"

"No, no! I have no wish to write. They have not heard for more than twenty years. It is no use writing now, they may all be dead."

"Oh, no, that is not probable. They will in time hear of the battle you have been in and see your name amongst the wounded. It would comfort them greatly to hear from you. If, as you say, you have not written for so long a time, how they would rejoice to find you had not forgotten them!"

"No, doctor," said Hubert, faintly, "it would be no joy to them; they cannot care for me now. I broke my mother's heart; I know it. I dreamt it once, years ago. Many a time the sad face I saw in my dream has come before me when I have least wanted it; many other things, too, doctor, I could tell you which forbid my writing. No, I cannot, at least not now - another time."

"No, my poor friend, not another time, write now: I'll write, shall I?"

"Write what and to whom? No, I tell you, they are dead;" and he turned his face away.

The Time for Reflection

The doctor knew well that Hubert's illness was too serious a matter to be trifled with. Everything was against him. It was the hottest season of the year, Dissipation had undermined his constitution and his mind was uneasy. The thought had struck that good man, that if he could get Hubert to turn his thought homeward, reflection might bring remorse for his past life and he might think of eternity. For a few seconds he stood still, gazing silently at his patient, wondering what he should do. It was not his custom to see a soldier die without feeling any concern. His own well-worn Bible testified how often he had used that sacred book. Written in the Book of Life were perhaps not a few names of erring, yet repentant sinners, brought to know Christ by his humble efforts. "Soldier brother," he said, as he took the hot hand once again in his own, "I must not be refused all I ask; let me read to you."

Hubert made no answer, and the doctor turned over the soiled pages of his Bible and read, with a soft, clear voice, the fifty-first Psalm -

"Have mercy upon me, O God, according to thy loving kindness; according unto the multitude of thy tender mercies blot out my transgressions..."

The psalm was ended. None of its petitions, however, appeared to have touched the heart of the sick man, though their effect was great upon the doctor, who, kneeling down, poured out his soul's grief in a deep, heartfelt prayer, begged hard and earnestly for mercy and pardon for his suffering brother and implored that a ray of light might beam into his heart. Never before had such a prayer sounded in Hubert's ear and yet, when the good man rose from his knees, the only sound that he heard was, "Doctor, I can sleep."

The Time for Reflection

"Goodnight, then," was the answer; "I shall come early in the morning and before then, if you require me; goodnight."

"Goodnight;" and there was a gentle pressure of the hand; then the doctor left the room.

"Is he gone?" said Hubert, faintly, a few minutes after. "Oh, why did he leave me" and the poor sufferer's eyes turned towards the door!?

The watcher that night was a woman. It was not often that a woman tended the sick soldiers in the hospital where Hubert now lay, but it was his lot to be so fortunate on this occasion. She was sitting beside an open window, looking out upon the sun, which was sinking in the west and throwing, as she was thinking, its rays upon her English home, when she heard Hubert speak. Hastening to his side in an instant, she asked him kindly if he required anything? Perhaps his heart was too full, for he only turned his head away and sighed deeply.

"Captain," she said, as she bent over him, "does anything trouble you? Can I get you anything?" And as she gently smoothed back the hair upon his forehead, she thought she saw a tear roll down his sun burnt cheek. That tear was enough; the stern scenes she had witnessed during a long sojourn in India had made her callous to many things and left many a scar upon her heart, but she was woman still and could not resist the power of that tear. She sat down upon the stool by the soldier's bed, chafed his hot hand in hers, cooled his brow again and again, and spoke soothingly and kindly to him. Still he was silent, gave no answer to any of her kind inquiries, except by an occasional sigh.

The Time for Reflection

"I know you are uneasy, Captain; tell me, oh, do tell me; I've asked you many things and you have answered me nothing; do tell me what's the matter. What can I do for you?"

"Nothing."

"Yes, Captain, let me do something; shall I fetch Dr. Martin? What shall I do?"

"Will you read to me?"

"Yes, that I will." The nurse immediately fetched her Bible and for a long time, by the dim flickering candle, her voice rose softly upon the stillness of that chamber, as she read of mercy and forgiveness to the penitent and heartbroken sinner.

It may have been that the sound of her voice had a soothing effect upon Hubert's ear, for he sunk calmly to sleep and his rest was peaceful. When he awoke, however, with the morning light, his pulse beat high, owing probably to the excitement of the previous day and the doctor was still unable to give hope of his recovery; After another day, when the shadows of evening drew on, that good man took his seat once more by the sufferer's bed and read again, in hopes to soothe the troubled spirit and lead the uneasy thoughts to better things.

"Why do you come here and sit and tire yourself reading to me? You must already be weary with your day's work, why do you come here?" And Hubert, with a steady eye, gazed into the doctor's face as he made the inquiry.

The Time for Reflection

"Why do I come?" Replied the doctor, as he gently took Hubert's hand, but he felt his throat swell at that moment and while he hesitated Hubert repeated, "Yes, why do you come?"

"Because it is my duty and because I have a deep affection for you. I am weary, but what matters that? You are more; so my necessity is not like yours and another thing, I know you are unhappy."

"Who told you?"

"I have not needed to be told; I know it well enough. You know I know it and for that cause I come to you, but the first thing I ask you, you refuse. You know not how great a comfort it would be to you to write home to your parents; there is much for you to do, but that is the first thing, for it is a holy duty."

"I have never done it, doctor, may God forgive me! I cannot do it now; it is too late, too late. You said right; I am not happy; the days and nights I have lain here, have told me that all is too late now. The life I have led has been a wicked one and if I die I am lost. Oh, what shall I do!?"

There was nothing stern in the doctor's heart. He had striven, wept and prayed earnestly that Hubert might see the error of his way. Now at this confession and despair, he almost regretted that he had added to the sufferer's woes. There was no exulting over the poor sinner, but bending down close to Hubert's ear, he said -

"Fear not; pour out your heart's sorrow to God; for, deep as your sins are, He can and will save you, if, with a true, penitent, and broken heart, you confess all your sins to Him and throw yourself helpless on his mercy. You can do nothing for yourself; your

The Time for Reflection

own poor, sorrowing heart is an offering Jesus Christ will accept if you will give it to him. Don't hesitate, Christ is waiting to receive you; do then, with godly sorrow, throw yourself upon His mercy."

"But I cannot," said Hubert. "It may be true all you say, but I have sinned so long, or else I am different than other people. God may forgive such as you, but I have sinned too much."

"Oh no, not too much for God to forgive. He knows all you have done and He knows all you need. Christ has died for you; why should you be lost?"

"Does God know all I've done? Does He know how hard I tried to lead a better life, and then Ellen died!? No, I cannot believe it. Go, go; leave me alone. What matters how I die? Go, and leave me as I am." Clasping his hands tightly upon his bosom, he said with earnestness, as he looked upward, "Lord, have mercy upon me." Then he was exhausted. A faint hue came over his face and the doctor, seeing that the strength of the sufferer was failing, stayed by his bedside to administer to his need. Hubert's hands had fallen upon the coverlet, and as the doctor took one in his own, he started at its strange coldness and for a long time he chafed it. All, indeed, that could be done, was done for Hubert and throughout the long, sultry, silent night, the nurse and doctor watched with Christian love beside the lonely bed. Hubert at length fell into a heavy sleep. It was the crisis of the fever and never was infant slumber more softly guarded than that of his. The next day went on; night came again; the sun in all its splendor went down in the western horizon and the doctor crept softly into Hubert's chamber to take another look at the sleeper. He had gazed some minutes. He had breathed a prayer and was turning away, when with a gentle sigh, Hubert awoke. There was

The Time for Reflection

a ray of light upon his face; he was better; the fever had left him. The doctor, after administering a cordial, gave him for the night to the care of the nurse, who well knew how to attend to him. He assured Hubert that, if he attended to his instructions, his leg would be the only cause or uneasiness and he hoped, by God's blessing, he would soon recover from that. Then, as he was leaving, he promised to come again the next morning and read to him. The morning came, the doctor was there and he told all about God's mercy and love to the vilest of earth's sinners; then he knelt and prayed with all the earnestness of his heart, for all God's grace to the sufferer, and with such simple words and touching sadness did he tell the Prodigal's story, that Hubert's unbelief and despair yielded at once to the mighty power of direct communication with God and tears fell fast upon his pillow.

The doctor had been more than an hour with Hubert and now onward to other sufferers he went, with his double mission. The scene in Hubert's room had urged him to be more earnest in his Master's cause and his soul was full of prayer that a heavenly ray might illumine Hubert's darkened heart and bring him to the feet of Jesus. Little did the sufferer know how earnestly that good man desired his salvation. Little did the regiment know, as its members saw him, with earnest thoughtful brow, wending his way beneath the shadow of the high wall, that in yonder lone building lay the cause of his toiling through the hot summer days. Toiling again as night came round, growing more sallow and more gaunt, yet never seeming to wary. "My grace is sufficient for thee," was strictly exemplified in that earnest faithful disciple; God blessed him and kept him a burning and a shining light, amidst all the sin and temptation of India's dark land. Though a scoff and a sneer were not infrequently the reward of his efforts to reclaim the sinner, many a scoffer sent for him in the last sad hour and a few testified, by a better life, to the holiness of his.

The Time for Reflection

Each time the doctor returned to Hubert, he found him slightly better. His wounded forehead was nearly well and his shattered leg was progressing favorably. All traces of feverishness were gone and the doctor seemed pleased as he told him that though at present the least thing might bring on fever again, which would certainly be fatal, yet, if all went well, he hoped in a few days to be able to pronounce him out of danger.

"Pray that it may be so," said Hubert, "for I dare not die now; God has heard your last prayer; a week ago I could have died to rid my heart of its dreadful despair, but not now. I do think there is a little hope for me - pray something for me, you know so well all about me - how came you to know so much?"

The doctor, sitting down by the bed, said, "Goodwin, many a year has passed away since you and your companions first attracted my notice. I remember well the morning you landed in Calcutta; for, if you recollect, your own doctor died on the passage out. I accepted the appointment as you lay out in the bay and went down to meet you on landing. I was, of course, strange to all of you, but the thing that struck me most was the extreme youth of the regiment - the majority did not appear much over twenty years of age. Then there were a good number of youths apparently about sixteen. I remember that many remarks were made at the time about you all and I came to the conclusion that at least half of you had come to India to die. I have not been wrong either in that, but I am going from the point - I remember that I was particularly struck with you and a fair, gentle-looking companion you had."

Hubert sighed, "It was poor Harris."

The Time for Reflection

"Yes, that was his name, poor fellow. Well, very soon I found out all about the life you were leading; your higher privileges were snares, not only to you and your companions, but also to all the men. The first grief I felt after joining you was at the reckless and sinful example you were setting. When first struck down with fever, how I longed, hoped and prayed for your conversion! But you know how your life passed on and I need not tell you that from that first hour of meeting you till now, I have watched you and prayed for you and I know quite well that God's Holy Spirit has often been striving very hard with you. But the warnings you have had have generally passed away like the dew upon the earth and now the Almighty has mercifully stopped your career by this affliction. Don't let it pass like the others have done, but take your heart with all its weight of sin and lay it bare before God. He knows all your needs, will help you in all your sorrows, pardon all your sins and make you holy, but you must ask His aid - you must confess all your sin - you must pray to Him with a broken heart."

Hubert sighed, and then, after a moment's pause, said, "Doctor, it is no easy matter to do as you say I ought. You judge me harshly when you say I have neglected all the warnings I have had. You remember poor Harris, well; his death had more effect upon me than you know. For weeks and weeks I thought of nothing else and tried very hard to change, but somehow I could not. And then poor Ellen! You remember her; I should have been another man if she had lived, but no, I was not allowed to be better: I lost her and I know I have been bad since; it drove me almost mad, but, Doctor, was it all my fault?" And Hubert burst into tears.

"Goodwin," said the doctor, as he took Hubert's hand, "beware how you rebuke the Almighty. His ways are not our ways; let me

The Time for Reflection

beg of you to have faith in Him now, if you are spared to recover, we will talk this point over together, but not now, time is too precious. Believe me, He does all things well and willeth not that any should perish. If you will only in true faith, nothing doubting, turn to Him, confess your sins and ask His mercy, you will be astonished how plain many things will appear that now seem dark and mysterious. Oh, do pray to Him!

"I have," said Hubert, softly: "I thought yesterday that I never could, but last night, after you were gone, some words I learnt once when a child came all into my mind. They seemed all I wanted to say and yet they were only part of a little child's prayer; indeed, I had long ago forgotten them - Doctor, will you pray?"

The good man knelt and poured out his heart to Heaven for the long sinning but repenting brother, and it was a holy sight to see the tears streaming down the pallid cheek of the once gay, reckless soldier, as he listened to another's prayer in his behalf. The doctor's bosom was full also - the wanderer was at last coming home - the straying sheep was returning to the fold - the poor child of earth was yielding up his proud spirit to the hand that afflicted, yet was stretched out to save him - and the good man prayed that the sufferer might be pardoned and spared to set forth the beauty of that holiness of life which he had so long neglected.

Another week had passed. Each day as it dawned found Hubert somewhat better, but then each evening both the nurse and doctor watched anxiously beside his bed, for his state was precarious. One thing, however, that improved was the state of his mind, that neither slumbered nor went back - but, from the hour that he poured out his first earnest heart-breathings to Heaven, he became more penitent and more anxious; all the

The Time for Reflection

carelessness and indifference with which he had treated religion came like so many accusing spirits before him, but, though the reflection of his past life helped at times to blanch his sunken cheek, he was more at peace in his bosom than he had been since his childhood.

Everything that could possibly be done for Hubert he received from the nurse and doctor. Their attentions were blessed, for at last Hubert was pronounced "out of danger;" and though he would never again be fit for the army, there were hopes of his perfect recovery.

CHAPTER VII

WHAT THE TORN BIBLE HAD DONE FOR HUBERT

I will throw off this dead and useless part, as a strong runner, straining for his life, unclasps a mantle to the hungry winds. - ALEXANDER SMITH

Five weeks more passed by, during which time Hubert grew in grace and his soul appeared to be ripening for heaven. His health improved and by the aid of a wheelchair he could be moved to the window of his room, where he sat for many an hour reading the Bible or enjoying the soft warm air as he gazed out upon the forests and jungle that lay before him, almost at his feet, or the snow-capped Himalayas in the distance.

One day as he sat by the window, he asked the nurse if she knew what became of the coat he wore on the day when he was wounded.

"Oh, yes, Captain," she replied, "I took care of it and put it away; if you wish to have it, I will fetch it for you."

"Thank you," said Hubert, "I should like to have it now." And the nurse went immediately to find it.

In a very few minutes the nurse returned and as she unfolded the coat, she said, "I fear it is very dirty, though these stains will be from the blood, I saw them when I folded it up, but I thought it best to take care of it, for I know soldiers generally prize the coat they were wounded in. I have sent many a one home to England

What the Torn Bible had Done for Hurbert

to the friends of those who have died - you will, I hope, be able to take your own."

"I hope so, nurse, though it will be some time yet before I can go," and then he began to examine the coat, and turned it over to find the pocket in the inside of the left breast: he found it, and there too was all that remained of his "torn Bible." Pale as his cheek was from pain and sickness, a deeper pallor came over it as he drew out the Bible and the cover of it met his eye. What was the meaning of the small round hole he saw? All the truth flashed upon his mind at once; he knew what it meant, and the cold perspiration stood out upon his forehead. With nervous hand, he turned over leaf by leaf until he came to a small bullet. It was not large but sufficient to have destroyed life if it had penetrated his heart. As he cast it upon the floor, he clasped the torn Bible to his bosom and bent his head low over his mother's last gift - that despised and neglected treasure.

The nurse had seen all that Hubert did upon receiving his coat. She saw him draw the book from the pocket, tremble as he opened it and then cast the bullet upon the floor. She would have taken but little notice of all that, if she had not seen his head droop as though something deeply troubled him.

"Come, Captain," she said, "that book makes you think sad things; come, sir, keep up your spirits and give me the book to keep till you are stronger."

"Don't touch it; leave it with me," said Hubert, pushing back her hand: "I am strong enough - go away."

"No, Captain. I must not go away; you are not strong enough to bear any excitement; it would just throw you back again, after all

What the Torn Bible had Done for Hurbert

our care of you. Think, sir, of getting well, not about that coat and book - I wish I had not brought them to you. I dare say when you see that coat all stained with blood and torn, you think about the narrow escape you have had: but cheer up Captain and don't think about it now."

"Look here," said Hubert, pointing to the cover of the book, "see what saved my life," and then he relieved his heart by telling her all about that book. As she listened she sat down upon a low chair before him and poor sympathizing one, she forgot, while her own tears fell as she heard the story he told, that she had, only a few minutes before, chided him for his sadness.

Three months had passed. Hubert's illness had been blessed to him. By the aid of crutches he moved about again and frequently encountered his old companions, some of them had visited him in hospital and there was a rumor in the regiment that Captain Goodwin had "gone religious." It caused some profane mirth amongst his comrades - the companions of his former life - and he felt ashamed to meet them. However, at last he did so and it was when they came around him and so warmly welcomed him back again and expressed their hope that he would soon be restored to perfect health, that he told them, with a holy boldness, that he regretted his past life and could never be one of their number again unless they gave up their evil ways and walked with him in the path of holiness. As might have been expected, the confession on the part of Hubert was received, for the most part, with laughter and derision. But his heart was set upon the thing he sought and from the hour he received the rebuff, he determined, if possible, to commence a work amongst his reckless companions. The same spirit of earnestness and devotion, which had helped Hubert in worldly advancement, marked his efforts now. He had partaken of heavenly things and

What the Torn Bible had Done for Hurbert

like a true disciple, could not bear the thought of any soul perishing. So, leaning upon his crutches, with his torn Bible in his hand, he went as often as his strength would allow. His own soul grew in grace as he told God's love to sinners, to his comrades. Hubert did not labor very long at his new work, his wounds had been too severe to allow of his continuing in the army and before another three months had passed, an order came for him to return to England.

At first, the idea of going back to his own country was not welcome, indeed India seemed to be his home more than England did and as he turned to the nurse, who still attended him, he said -

"Nurse, I shall not go to England. How can I go with this poor useless leg? I had better stay here."

"But, Captain, your leg is not useless; the doctor says you may some day be able to walk with a stick."

"Does he? I will be very long first, I fear. No, I think I shall not go home, no one will know me, for it is not as though I went home all right."

"Bless you, sir," replied the nurse, "plenty will know you - your mother will for one. I remember when our Tom ran away and went to sea and was gone ten years. We never heard a word about him until all at once, home he came and the moment we caught sight of him at the garden gate, though he had grown from a boy to a stout man, we all cried out, 'Here's poor Tom!' We had never heard a word about his coming or anything, yet we knew him and all ran out to meet him. I remember it well how poor mother threw her arms round his neck and kissed him and

What the Torn Bible had Done for Hurbert

called him her darling. I can't tell you how she stood and cried and scolded him for running away and never writing and then how she took up her apron to wipe away her tears and then kissed and hugged him again. I never shall forget it. Poor mother! She and Tom are in heaven now. I watched beside them both and though my heart nearly broke when I lost them, I had rather have them where they are than enduring the trials of this life."

"Did your brother die soon after he returned, then?" inquired Hubert.

"He only lived three years after he came home, for he had been very much beaten about and his health was quite broken. Poor mother died six months before he did. The year after they died, I married and came out here and I have seen some trouble. I buried three little children, one after another, and then I buried my husband. They all lay just out there, under that large tree in the corner of the burial-ground. I was ordered home, but I could not leave the spot where they were lying and so gave up my passage to England and have stayed here ever since. I have only one wish and that is to be buried just out there beside them. It is sixteen years since my husband died, and the first time you can get so far, just go and see how nicely I keep his and the children's graves."

Hubert was interested in the woman's story, her patient devotion and affection won his heart and he took the first opportunity of visiting the graves of her loved ones. As he gazed upon the well-kept mounds before him, his thoughts sped over the ocean to a distant land and he saw the village churchyard, with the grassy hillocks beneath which lay the remains of many members of his family. And lifting up his heart in prayer to God for humility and

What the Torn Bible had Done for Hurbert

strength, he determined to bid farewell to India and return to the fold from which he had wandered.

It was soon known that Hubert was going to England and many ready hands and hearts assisted him in preparing to go. All his little property was collected, several presents were given him, and many a regret was expressed at his leaving, all of which made it harder to go than he had anticipated. He felt, as the time drew near, more and more sorry to leave. But there was no alternative; so he decided to sail in the first vessel that left Calcutta after he arrived there. The doctor, to whom Hubert had communicated his intention, came to him one evening and told him, that as he was at liberty to choose his own vessel, he could not do better than make his passage over the seas in the *Arctic*. "She is a splendid ship," said the doctor, "and the captain is a religious man. I know him well. You will not be annoyed with riotous conduct in his vessel and will have no cause to complain of the manner in which he observes the Sabbath."

"Ah, that will be the ship, then," replied Hubert, "but did you ever sail in it?"

"Yes, twice to the Cape of Good Hope and back. I can assure you that I have been in many a church and have not heard the service with such comfort as I heard it in that ship. Our beautiful Liturgy was read with such deep earnestness and pathos that I thought then and I have thought ever since, that out on the ocean, with dangers around us, is the fittest place for those grand prayers to be breathed. For as I joined and listened, I thought I could see Christ beside me walking upon the sea, and my soul seemed carried up higher into heaven than it had ever been before."

What the Torn Bible had Done for Hurbert

"That was beautiful!" exclaimed Hubert; "I always like to hear you talk like that, doctor, it makes me feel something of the same kind. I shall like that ship, when will she sail?"

"I scarcely know, but it will not be long. She has been lying at Calcutta some time and I should think is about returning to England. She has not gone, I know, because Lieutenant White told me last night that he intended sending a box to England by her. By the way, he can perhaps tell us when she will sail."

It was found, upon inquiry, that the *Arctic* would set sail in about ten days; so Hubert bade farewell as soon as he could to his friends and accompanied by the doctor, was in a few days on his way to Calcutta. He bore the fatigue of the journey better than he had expected, though he was very much exhausted and was heartily glad when he reached the ship and lay down to rest in his cabin. The doctor stayed all night and then the next morning they took leave of each other, promising to continue the friendship, which, to Hubert at least, had been such a blessing. Hubert did not at first feel all he had lost when the doctor left, for his mind was somewhat occupied in arranging his cabin, so as to be as comfortable as possible on the voyage. But this, of course, had an end and a consciousness came over him that he was friendless on the wide world amongst strangers. At first he thought it would be better to keep so and not leave his cabin at all, for, if he went on deck, the remarks or sympathy of the other passengers would be very annoying. They might pity him and be kind and attentive to him in his weakness, but it would only make him feel more keenly the calamity, which had fallen on him in the full vigor of his manhood. His thoughts rushed back and he saw himself but a few months before so full of health and activity. He forgot the great blessing that had accompanied his illness, and his heart murmured and rebelled. A dark cloud seemed to have

What the Torn Bible had Done for Hurbert

fallen over Hubert. For three days he maintained a gloomy silence in his cabin. The sailor that waited upon him told his shipmates that it was a pity his honor had chosen the sea for a grave for unless he changed, he would, in his honest opinion; die before they were far out of the bay. "Tell him so Ben, for you know it ain't lucky to have a death on board," said one of the sailors. However, Ben said nothing to Hubert, for in his own mind he began to think that the soldier had a sorrow, which would perhaps wear away in time and the sailor was not wrong. It was a dark hour in Hubert's life - a weak yielding of the flesh and who can wonder? In the short time that had passed since he had given up his evil ways, how much instruction and counsel he had received from the kind friend who had brought him to the vessel, and the kind nurse, so full of sympathy towards him, knowing all about him, had helped to buoy up his spirits when they were sinking. By them, the struggle between his old and his new nature had been lightened. How Hubert missed those two friends now! He never thought he could have cared for them half so much. In the gloomy thoughts that had come over him, he would have given much for one of them to have been near, but he was alone, and his nature warred with his spirit, and his bosom refused to be comforted. Many times he wished he could return to India and reproached himself for having left. There at least, was someone that cared for him; now, where was he? Out on the sea, without a friend, and perhaps, in the distant land to which he was going he might find himself friendless still. Friendless! The thought bowed him very low but God knew the storm that was beating upon the heart of the returning wanderer and the powerful hand of Omnipotence tempered the hurricane. For like the distant sound of help in the lull of the tempest, the words came suddenly into his mind - "I will never leave thee, nor forsake thee."

What the Torn Bible had Done for Hurbert

"Ah!" said Hubert, starting and pointing upward as he spoke, "Gracious God, I have a friend in thee;" then, clasping his hands together, he prayed an earnest prayer that God would pardon the sin of his murmuring, help him to overcome the evil nature in his heart and make him more holy.

Hubert's peace of mind returned as soon as he had poured out his grief in prayer and Ben the sailor told his shipmates that they need not fear now for his Honor had taken a turn and was quite cheerful like. The evening of another day was closing, and Hubert came upon deck amongst the other passengers, to take a last look of the land where the best years of his life had been passed and where nearly all the remembered associations of his existence were centered.

The home of his boyhood, in that lovely English valley, had come before him in memory's brightest colors, as he lay sick and wounded in the hospital. He thought of it too when he set out for England, but he could remember nothing at all of it as he stood by the side of the vessel, looking back upon his manhood's home - the field of his fame. It was true that he had there strayed further from the right path and sunk deeper into sin; that, if India had been the scene of his fame, it had also been the scene of his guilt. But then his heart whispered that it was there too he had mourned and repented and if a deep sigh escaped his bosom, as he watched the last shadow of his Indian home fade from his view, it was because he was leaving it forever.

Long after the last look had been taken, Hubert sat still upon deck, and was roused from his thoughtfulness by the words -

"Will you accept my arm, Captain, to your cabin, it is getting late?"

What the Torn Bible had Done for Hurbert

"Thank you, I had forgotten, I see it is late. I can manage pretty well with my crutch, but no, since you kindly offer me your arm, I will accept it."

"Yes, do, Captain, the vessel is not over steady."

When Hubert reached his cabin, he turned his head to thank his friend and then he saw that he was a man many years older than himself, with a clear open countenance and with hair deeply tinged with grey.

"You are welcome," said the stranger and I hope we shall become better acquainted, for we have a long voyage before us, which I, like you, appear to be making alone and pleasant society will render it cheerful - goodnight."

"Goodnight," replied Hubert; "I hope it will be as you say," and grasping his hand, he again said, "Goodnight."

They were now far out at sea. The high lands of India had sunk below the horizon. Ceylon, with its spicy perfumes was passed and Adam's Peak, the high towering sentinel of that wonderful island, had sunk also beneath the wave. Hubert enjoyed the sea. His health and spirits returned and the time passed much more pleasantly than he had anticipated. He found his new friend a most agreeable companion, kind and considerate towards him and having been a great traveler, he was ever ready and willing to amuse Hubert. Not only with accounts of the countries to which he had traveled, but also of England, which country he had left only five years before. He had been a wanderer all his life. He was born upon the sea in his father's vessel, and being early deprived of his mother, he and his brother became the

What the Torn Bible had Done for Hurbert

companions of all their father's voyages. Born, as it were, to a wandering life, a life which in after years they were in no way fitted to give up, his brother succeeded to the command of his father's ship, while he roamed to nearly every part of the world and gave to society many valuable volumes of information on different parts of the earth and its people.

Hubert always listened with pleasure to the conversation of his friend. Still there was ever a wish in his mind that the subject would change. He longed to hear him talk of higher things than those of earth, for never once, in all he said, did he make reference to the God of heaven. It seemed to be the God of this world that he worshipped and Hubert sighed as he thought that he had not proved the true friend he had hoped to find in him.

CHAPTER VIII

HOMEWARD BOUND

Back to the world we faithless turn'd, and far along the wild, with labor lost and sorrow earn'd, our steps have been beguiled. - KEBLE

The Sundays on board the *Arctic* were spent as the doctor had led Hubert to expect. Happy, holy days they were, no one enjoyed them more than Hubert. On more than one occasion he spoke of them to his friend. His remarks, however, were never responded to heartily and Hubert felt annoyed that he had formed a friendship with a man who seemed to have no interest in the chief of all his enjoyments. "It may be" said Hubert one day, as he sat alone in his cabin - "it may be because he has never been struck down as I have been, or it may be - Ah! What may it be?" Then he fell into a deep reverie, and wondered many things as to the cause of his friend's indifference to sacred things. He prayed for a beam of light into the heart, which appeared to him to be darkened. Hubert felt a growing anxiety about his friend. He knew they could not be companions very long. The journey, long as it yet was, was daily growing shorter and he did not feel certain that he would not be in some way responsible if he allowed the present opportunity to pass.

Some timid Christians are frightened into silence by the mere worldly boldness of those amongst whom they dwell, but it was not so with Hubert. His companion was a quiet, unobtrusive man, as amiable and kind as it was possible to be and yet Hubert had not boldness sufficient to tell him that the Bible was the theme he loved best and heaven the chief place of his interest.

Homeward Bound

And why was it? In that stranger there was education, refined taste and eloquence, united to the pursuits of a lifetime. Whatever resolution Hubert made when alone, he always failed to accomplish it when he came and sat down by his side. Sometimes, the subject was upon Hubert's lips and many times his hand was in his coat pocket, in which the torn Bible lay, but then he feared to produce it, lest his friend, who seemed to know the human heart so well, should reproach him for having taken up religion in his infirmity, when he had devoted his health and strength to dissipation and pleasure. It grieved him very much, for it made him ill at ease with himself, His Bible was his chief companion, it is true and there was nothing more that he loved so well. Sometimes he wondered at himself for taking such delight in it and acting upon the advice of his old friend the doctor, "to try and examine all the thoughts and intentions of the heart," he imposed upon himself many a search to find out, if possible, why it was that the pages of that torn book gave him such delight. Why, at times, his tears would fall as he read it and why sometimes, his bosom would swell and his heart beat, at the story it told him. But he could not find out how it was, he only knew that he loved it and wanted others to love it too.

The ship made a rather quick run to the Cape, where she stayed a fortnight. Hubert improved so much in strength that he laid aside his crutch and walked easily with two walking sticks. With his returning strength, his spirit and face grew more cheerful and he began to feel a hankering for his home in England. It became a favorite thought and after that a frequent topic of conversation.

"I have only one desire," he would sometimes say, "and that is, that those I left behind so many years ago may be alive to welcome me home."

Homeward Bound

"You can hardly expect it," said his friend on one occasion, as they sat together on deck. "A great many changes occur in the space of a quarter of a century and it is generally those we love best who are taken the first away from us."

"Perhaps to draw our thoughts to heaven," said Hubert.

"Perhaps so," replied his friend, "but suppose it does not do it and instead of our becoming very resigned and heavenly-minded we become reckless and desperate and think of any place but heaven, - what then?"

"I don't know," said Hubert, "except that the man who could feel what you say must be one who has forgotten to worship God and so when trouble comes upon him he hasn't God to help him to bear it."

The stranger looked earnestly into Hubert's face. There might have been a home-thrust in that remark, for heaving a deep sigh, he said, "I hope you have never known what it is to lose a friend very, very dear to you and I hope you never will - yours is a beautiful delusion. I had it once but I haven't it now and I hope circumstances may never rob you of it."

"I hope not, but my friend," said Hubert, laying his hand upon his arm, "I *have* lost one very, very dear to me, all I ever loved, and it is the beautiful delusion you name that has helped me to bear it. Nay, it is not a delusion, it is a high hope. A hope that when this life is ended and all who are dear to us have been taken away, we shall meet once again in heaven, to live together forever."

Homeward Bound

Hubert's face had become animated while he spoke and in his warmth he put his hand into his pocket, intending to bring out his Bible but his friend checked him by saying, "what a strange, powerful influence the things we learn in our youth have over our lives! A holy precept instilled into us when we are lads, is a diamond set in a imperishable casket and though the dust of careless, skeptical manhood may oftentimes cover over the gem, still it is there as bright as ever, ready to shine with its former luster when the heart, trusting and believing, instead of doubting, fans off the black shadow of unbelief. Surely it is then that God's Spirit breathes once again into man the breath of life."

"How I wish I could talk as you do!" said Hubert. "Then I would tell you what I feel. But when I want to speak, I seem to feel so much that I have no words to express myself and so I say but little. How is it though, that you speak so of God? I thought you were unbelieving?"

"And what have I said to make you think that I believe now?"

"You must," said Hubert, "else you would not speak so of the Spirit of God. When I spoke of God, you called it a delusion and I said nothing like what you have said. You surely are not a skeptic: you must believe."

"I may believe some things, but not all that you do. For it has been an easy matter to forget all about the one true God in a country where so many gods are worshipped."

"Did you forget, with all your learning and eloquence? Did *you* forget?"

"Yes; didn't you?"

Homeward Bound

"Oh yes, I did; I dare not tell you what I did, neither can I tell you what I have suffered, nor how good and gracious God has been to me. For more than twenty years I chose to live regardless of a future life. Indeed, regardless of anything but sin. I always tremble when I think how I have lived and yet see how gracious God has been to me. Although you, too, forget to serve Him, He has not forgotten to be gracious and merciful to you."

The stranger sat still, in a careless attitude, with his broad-brimmed straw had shading his face, and his hands thrust into the pockets of his loose coat. He spoke nothing in answer to Hubert's remarks and Hubert, after maintaining the silence for some time, rose from his seat and went to his cabin. Ben, the sailor, had opened the cabin window, against which the rippling of the calm sea occasionally threw a tiny crystal and as Hubert entered and saw Ben standing before the window, he said -

"Are you afraid the water will be in, Ben?"

"Oh no, your honor," said the sailor, touching the little bit of hair upon his forehead, "we're more than four feet above water at this window, but I was a thinking, your honor, of the storm on the Sea of Galilee and how our Savior caused a great calm. It was a wonderful thing and I dare say it made a good many believe on Him as didn't believe before. St. Mark says there was also some little ships besides the one Christ was in and I dare say there was a good many in those ships as didn't believe Him at all, but it just wanted that great tempest to frighten 'em and make 'em believe."

"It might indeed," replied Hubert, into whose heart a new light had suddenly shone, "for God, who knows all hearts, knew what was in theirs."

Homeward Bound

"True, your honor, and it's the same now; many men won't believe the Gospel until they are like as it were in the tempest, obliged to be struck down with illness, or such like, I mean."

With the concluding words, the sailor left the cabin and Hubert sat down to read all about that storm on the Sea of Galilee. He had read it before but never with such an interest as now. It reminded him of the tempest that had once come upon him and he saw a deep truth in the sailor's remark, that it is the storm that drives the sinner to Christ. Then he sat and wondered what he must do to try and convince his stranger friend of these things and the prayer was almost upon his lips that some terrible tempest might overwhelm him, if it would bring him to the footstool of Jesus.

That night, as though in answer to his heart's desire, Hubert dreamt that his friend was "a vessel meet for the Master's use," and in a joyous burst of feeling he awoke.

"I know it, I am sure of it," he said to himself, "he is a believer; a backslider, perhaps, but not a skeptic." And he longed for the daylight to come, that he might again seek his friend. As he lay awake during the remainder of the night, he tried to throw many of the incidents of his own life round that of the stranger. He would give anything almost, to hear something more of his history. What he had told him was not enough and Hubert hoped for a closer and firmer friendship. A kindred wish seemed to have passed nearly at the same time through the mind of the stranger, for he had retired to rest with the hope that he might get to know something more of Hubert. The next morning, when they met on deck, there was a cordial greeting and they went and sat down on the seat they had occupied the day before. There were several passengers on board the ship but Hubert and the

Homeward Bound

stranger were exclusive in their friendship, so that when together, they met with no interruption. This time, as they talked of various things, with the widespread ocean around them, Hubert, after a pause, said -

"Did you ever read the story of Jesus Christ stilling the tempest on the Sea of Galilee?"

"Yes, many times; why?"

Then Hubert repeated what Ben the sailor had said; told, too, from whose honest heart the ideas came, and his bosom felt a thrill of pleasure at the earnest attention the stranger gave him.

"Well done Ben," burst suddenly from his lips.

"Why, Captain Goodwin, he's a clearheaded fellow. It's astonishing what remarkably good notions those sailors sometimes have."

Then he returned to Hubert's subject. He painted in rich imagery the silent lake, the little vessels and the sleeping Savior. Then the tempest, the alarm, the cry, "Save, or we perish," and the Omnipotent, "Peace, be still." He knew all about it. He likened the silent lake to man's heart in boasted security; the little vessels to the many sins of his indulgence. The sleeping Savior to conscience hushed by sin. The tempest, to man awakening. The alarm, to man seeking pardon. The cry, to man's heart broken in despair and the "Peace, be still," the voice of a reconciled God, the sign manual of forgiveness.

Homeward Bound

Hubert had never heard anything that told upon his heart with stronger power. Tears were in his eyes and drawing a long breath, he said -

"How could you make me think that there was anything that you did not believe in reference to God, when you know so much and can explain so beautifully? Oh, if I knew only half what you do - if I had but a little of your power to express myself, what a Christian I would be."

"You don't know," said the stranger, laying his hand upon Hubert's raised arm. "The head may be full of knowledge and the tongue fluent in speech and yet the heart may be cold. It has been said, that for a speaker to move the hearts of his hearers, he must himself feel the power of his subject. Now, in worldly matters it may be so, but I am inclined to think that in religious matters it is not obliged to be. There is in all things referring to man's soul a secret influence that does not necessarily require the fire of man's heart to make it effective. God's Spirit is alone sufficient to move the waters. Eloquence, indeed! Oh, beware how you covet it. Where is there anything finer than the testimony of Christ's divinity made by the *demon* in the synagogue at Capernaum - 'What have we to do with thee, thou Jesus of Nazareth? Art thou come to destroy us? I know thee who thou art, the Holy One of God.' Be assured, that after all, there is no sublime strain that reaches the ears of the Most High, than the contrite 'Lord, save, or we perish.'"

There was much earnestness in the stranger's manner and the last words he uttered struck Hubert as a prayer coming up from the depths of that heart which, in the stillness of the previous night, he had satisfied himself that he was not skeptical, but backsliding. Hubert's curiosity was more awakened and just as he was about

Homeward Bound

to ask his friend another question, they were interrupted by the sailors coming to the part of the vessel where they were seated, to attend to some portion of the rigging. Hubert, taking his stick, walked away slowly to his cabin, but his friend did not follow him and he sat down in silence alone. How many subjects, during the voyage that stranger had given Hubert to think about! The time had passed so pleasantly, that he had not missed quite so much as he had anticipated, the friends in India. Many new lights had shone into his heart and his mind had opened to more truths by the companionship he had made. He felt now as much delighted with the friendship, as a short time before he had been disappointed. That short prayer, so emphatically spoken, had touched a deep feeling of his own heart and he wondered whether the high order of intellect, the learning and eloquence of his friend, had not proved to him a snare, in the same way that the careless, reckless, self-will of his own nature had been to him.

"Great God!" he said, gazing upward, "guide the thoughts of my heart aright, lest I argue that some of thy gifts are given to man to his injury."

How humble Hubert had become. How ready to resign his own will to that of a higher! Many a prayer he breathed that day, for the evil thought came continually up in his mind that God's gifts were not always for good. Do as he would, or think as he would, that same thought was uppermost in his mind and he felt that it was the evil one grasping at the expiring hope of bringing him back to him again. Hubert's faith, however, was growing stronger every day. He had learnt to feel that without the guidance and protection of God, he was a frail erring creature. It led him to be frequently a suppliant and frequently a receiver of heavenly strength.

Homeward Bound

"Get thee behind me Satan! Every gift of God is good and perfect and it is thou, thou false one, that perverts them from the end for which they are given." Hubert, as he ceased speaking, took out his "torn Bible" to read. There was comfort there and his heart became more cheerful, his faith stronger, as he read upon a soiled torn page of that precious book - "Fear thou not, for I am with thee; be not dismayed, for I am thy God: I will strengthen thee; yea, I will help thee; yea, I will uphold thee with the right hand of my righteousness."

It mattered not to whom, nor under what circumstances, such passages of Scripture were written. They were as effective to Hubert as though they had been penned for him alone. He took them all to himself and became more trusting and more holy. Neither Jew nor Gentile made a stone at which his feet were to stumble. As he opened his "torn Bible" and read, so he believed: the promise or the threatening, as it stood there, was what his heart received and he believed now that God was near him, helping him to overcome the tempter.

CHAPTER IX

TRUE FRIENDSHIP

Then, potent with the spell of heaven, go, and thine erring brother gain; entice him home to be forgiven, till he, too, see his Saviour plain. - KEBLE

Three weeks more passed away; the journey homeward was getting near its end, for the weather had been fine, and, except that on account of a death on board, the vessel stayed a day and a night at St. Helena, there were no interruptions. It was a lovely morning, the wind was hushed, there was scarcely a ripple upon the ocean, the vessel glided on without breaking the stillness, and Hubert sat on deck with his friend, enjoying the genial atmosphere of the temperate zone.

"Captain Goodwin," said the traveler, "I think our journey together is nearly ended."

"Are you not going to England?" Hubert inquired immediately.

"No - at least, not at present. In a few days we shall pass Portugal and I may say farewell to you off Lisbon. I have a little matter on hand that takes me to that part; when I have finished it, I hope to come to England and I hope to meet you some day again. I trust that what we have seen of each other has not been unprofitable; something I have told you may remain in your memory, for I have told you many things concerning the ways of men in nearly every country that I have been to. Your knowledge has been confined to India, which country I have traversed almost from one end to the other. Yet I have learnt very much

True Friendship

from you and now that we are about to part, I will tell you how. It may be that, mixing so much amongst Indian idolatry or indeed, I hardly know what has been the cause - but of late years I have grown careless of the pure faith of my childhood and have rather liked than otherwise, anything that tended to increase a disbelief in God and a future life. Once let the thought that there is not a future fix itself in the mind of a man and a thousand other thoughts more wicked than the first follow. There is little difficulty in disbelieving altogether, for it is the belief that there is a future that constitutes the keystone in religion. Well, I had become skeptical and Goodwin, you perhaps little thought it, but it was you with your Bible and all its precepts so exemplified in your conduct that struck me and made me look into my own heart to find how it was that you appeared so much more happy and contented than I was. I have often watched you and your silent, as you thought, unseen study of your Bible, had a powerful effect upon me and did more for me than any noisy demonstration would have done. When I first met with you, I was in a state of mind to have laughed at you, if you had come and talked about conversion and grace and prated off a host of Scripture texts. I had too long forsaken religion to be frightened back to it and that is the mistake many good people make in their endeavors to bring back God's wandering children. When I saw you so consistent and so earnest in your religious duties I knew this, that I longed to be like you and that longing led me to think of what I had once been and by degrees, things have changed with me. I have wanted to tell you this before, but have always been afraid to trust myself; it is because our journey is so nearly ended that I tell you now, and look here, Goodwin; when I have done what I have to do in Portugal I will come to England, where I shall hope to meet you, and by God's blessing, since there is no secret between us now, we will talk this matter over again. It may

True Friendship

be a year before I come, perhaps longer, but remember, if I am spared, I will come, for I shall never forget you."

"Neither shall I you," said Hubert, grasping his hand, but his heart was full and for some minutes he said no more; at length he continued, "Oh, I am sorry to part with you, I have often wished that some of our time could be spent in reading God's word and talking of his mercy to us both. The want of our doing so has made me at times sadly miss two friends I left in India. Still, I have much enjoyed your society and have learned very much from you. For though our conversation has for the most part been upon secular things, you have given me very much to think about and I thank God that I met with you. When I reach home," and Hubert sighed, "I should like to write to you and if you will tell me where a letter will find you I will do so. I shall take up my quarters in the north of England."

The traveler gave Hubert an address, which he said, would find him, at least for the next three months and then he added:

"The north of England! Ah! I well remember an incident that occurred once as I passed through it on my way from Edinburgh to London. I have never been in that part since and as near as I can recollect, it is about four-and-twenty years ago. I was fifty-four years old yesterday and I was thinking that I passed my thirtieth birthday on the top of that stagecoach. Well, we were some distance north of York - I have forgotten the name of the place, but it was a charming little village. At the top of a shady lane, at the garden-gate of a pretty house, there were several people waiting to bid a young soldier goodbye. Young indeed! He was only a lad, just fifteen, a fine-hearted sprightly young fellow and he was going off to India! Well, he took his seat amongst the passengers, called out goodbye and off we went. I

True Friendship

sat beside the coachman and as I glanced at him, I felt sorry for the boy, for, though he appeared cheerful enough, I had an idea that his cheerfulness was a little forced. The passengers began to talk with him and he really was a fine fellow. I never shall forget him - the very type of a handsome English youth. Excuse me, I was forgetting myself, it's but a simple story after all, we can find something better to talk about."

"Oh no, pray finish it, I am interested in your story. What became of the young soldier?"

"Well, it was rather curious that I was going south on purpose to bid my brother goodbye and I found that this young soldier was going to India in my brother's ship."

"That was curious enough," said Hubert.

"It was, and when we alighted after a long and tedious journey to London, we went off to the ship together. How very often I have thought of that lad. He had evidently been well cared for by good religious parents, but perhaps from his school training or I cannot tell what, he was certainly forgetting the instructions they had given him. Oh, how thoughtless and reckless he was! I watched him, for he had told us a little of his history and as I was leaving the ship; I ventured to give him a word of advice and tried to persuade him never to forget his duty to his parents. I cannot tell you more about him. Poor lad! I never saw him again, nor ever heard of him after he reached India. I fear he died, for soon after his regiment landed, many of the soldiers died of fever and from what I can remember, I saw amongst the deaths in an Indian paper a soldier of his name; so, never hearing anything more of him, I concluded the poor fellow had succumbed to the climate."

True Friendship

"Why were you so anxious to hear something more of that lad in particular?" inquired Hubert.

"Ah! Were I to tell you, it would be a long story. I don't know, though, that I need tell all. I think I once told you some of my early history. Well, I married at an early age and three years after my marriage, I buried my wife. The sorrow, however, was greatly alleviated by a little son I had - he was two years old when his mother died and just able to dissipate my grief by his innocent prattle. Years passed away: wherever I went I took my boy. I traveled through Germany and Prussia with him and it has often occurred to me that the many people, who have been charmed by the works that these travels helped to produce, little thought under what circumstances they were accomplished. Many a long journey, where conveyances could not go, have I taken, with my staff in hand, a little satchel at my side, and that boy on my back. At other times he has trotted by my side, and very often - most nights, indeed - with him sleeping in my arms or seated beside his bed, I have penned most of my daily wanderings, for I never left him. For eight years after his mother died I never allowed him to go from my sight, but then he left me for ever."

"Not for ever," said Hubert; "you mean he died, well, you will go to him, though he will not return to you."

"Why do you say so?"

"Because I believe it and so do you."

"Yes, I do: but now, tell me how it is that I cannot always think so. I believe it all as well as you do and yet, when I sit alone and

True Friendship

think, my thoughts are not the same as when we sit and talk together - how is it?"

There was earnestness in the stranger's manner and also in his eye, as he put this question to Hubert, who, after sitting unmoved for a minute or two, at last said:

"I have felt the same way many, many times. Indeed, there is scarcely a truth in the Bible that I have read, which, though I believed it at one time, I have been led to doubt it another. Many a time have I gone out into the courtyard of my quarters in India, that I might see some fresh object, because upon everything in my room there seemed to stand out in large gilded letters the word '*Unbelief*'; turn where I would, sometimes the very objects and things I wished to forget were always before my eyes. Indeed, blasphemy has been upon my tongue, when my heart has dictated prayers. Terrible hours they have been to me and sometimes the falling of a piece of paper, the opening of a door, or the smallest possible sound you could conceive, has so alarmed me, that I have actually been afraid of myself. No one but myself can know what I endured but I don't feel anything of the sort now. *Prayer* was the effectual remedy for me and it will be so for you. I believe that such doubts and fears are extra mercies sent by God to bring us nearer to Him. So, when you feel anything of the kind, try what prayer will do. There is a great deal of seeming prayer that isn't prayer, but when the heart can feel itself going out upwards, - I mean, when it utters the words, 'Lord, I believe, help thou mine unbelief', depend upon it, that upon the other side of the petition, written in words of fire, is the command to the tempter, 'Get thee behind me, Satan!' "

The stranger sighed but then, thrusting his hands deeply into his coat pockets, as was his usual custom when in a thoughtful

True Friendship

mood, he sat still looking over upon the broad blue sea. Hubert sat still beside him, and, as the sailors moved about attending to their various duties, they gave many a glance at the two friends as they sat together. Ben had told them all something about these friends and though they were not all of the same way of thinking as Ben was, they imbibed from him an extra amount of respect for the Captain and the stranger, and had the part of the deck were they were accustomed to sit been a sacred part, it could not have been more free from intrusion than it was when they were there. So Hubert sat and thought, as did his friend, who was the first to speak:

"Yes, it is so," he said. "I know it is all true, I shall go to *them*. And now let me finish my story. I had returned from the Continent and it was in Scotland that I buried my son; he was laid beside his mother in the kirk-yard at Dunkeld. It is a pretty, quiet place, at the foot of the Grampian mountains, and there they lie - I hope to be buried there too some day. I did not think at the time that I should have lived thus long after them, but time has fled on and it has worked its change in me. I remember that it was on my first journey after my loss that that lad rode with us to London. I shall never forget how startled I was when I first saw him. Older, of course, he was, but such an exact resemblance did he bear to the one I had lost, that - it may have been a delusion - some of my affection for the dead seemed to centre in him."

"What was his name?" inquired Hubert.

"I cannot tell now, I had forgotten it long ago; indeed, I had forgotten the incident until you brought it back to my memory, it happened so long ago."

True Friendship

"I wonder you forgot his name, though," said Hubert, "but time works upon the memory, and makes it less retentive."

"True; especially one that has been tried like mine has. I am not an old man - I am only a little over fifty, yet see how grey I am, I attribute it to my memory being over-tasked."

"And to early and deep sorrow, perhaps," replied Hubert.

"Well, the philosophy of that I neither argue nor dispute; what do you say to it?"

Hubert smiled, and taking from his pocket his torn Bible, he said, "Here we have a high authority for the fact that suffering purifies the heart. Now, whatever effect it may have upon the outward appearance, it most certainly leaves its impress within - leaves many a deep scar upon the heart - and we know that it leaves furrows on the brow; yet what a blessing suffering is! It is often the last effort that God makes to reclaim the reckless sinner. When all other efforts have failed and nothing seems effectual in bringing down man's proud heart, the Almighty smites, that He may bless. I know it, for I have experienced it all; I have felt both the scourge and the blessing."

Hubert added this latter part because he feared lest his friend should think him presumptuous, but the stranger added, "Captain Goodwin, I am sure you must have felt a good deal of what you have often talked about and I would give much to be always as thoroughly settled in these matters as you are. What you say, I feel to be all perfectly true; here," he said, placing his hand upon his heart, "it is all right, but here," and he touched his forehead, "there are other thoughts, but if God spare me, I will come to you again when my business in Portugal is done and then we will

True Friendship

talk over these matters more fully. The world has been a wide one to me, but I have only a few friends in it and am tired of rambling about it, so I shall return to England and come near to you."

"Do," said Hubert, "and may God spare you and me too. I shall be glad indeed to see you, the heart grows better by communion and I think somehow that there is many a kindred feeling between us.
At any rate, our voyage has been rendered pleasant by our having met and it will be a source of pleasure to me, in many a sad hour that I feel will yet befall me, to look forward to our meeting again."

This, and much more, formed the matter for conversation between Hubert and his friend, and when the day had closed and night drew on, they passed an hour together by Hubert's lamp, for the heart which had unburdened itself seemed to have twined its tendrils more firmly round the wounded soldier.

CHAPTER X

THE WANDERER'S RETURN

*Lead, kindly light, amid the evening gloom, lead thou me on!
The night is dark, and I am far from home: lead thou me on!* - KEBLE

Nearer and nearer drew the vessel homeward. Hubert and his friend had that morning kept below, there was little luggage on a table upon the deck and two or three people were standing near it. Some of the sailors were evidently busy about one of the boats but a casual observer could not have perceived that anything unusual was going on. Many, nearly all in the vessel, were gladdening their eyes with the first glimpse they were having of Europe, and as the coast of Portugal became more distinct, many hearts burst out with joy, for they were nearing home.

Hubert and his friend at length came on deck; Lisbon, with its noble bay and high lands, could be seen in the distance, and the boat was lowered to convey the passengers to the small vessel that would take them up the river to the town. "Farewell!" It was the last word from Hubert's lips that sounded upon the traveler's ears as he was wafted over the billows that rolled upon the shores of Portugal; "Farewell!" echoed back upon the air, and Hubert, drawing a deep sigh, began already to feel lonely. He had made no other friend in the ship and he returned to his cabin. He sat down and began to think over the conversations he had had with his friend and he wondered again and again whether he himself was not indeed that once reckless boy, who in years gone by had won the sympathies of the noble heart, which had now won his. So many incidents in that short narrative had a counterpart in his memory, that at last nothing could persuade him but that it all referred to himself. Then, how sorry he felt that he had not told his friend more about himself, and, less at ease than he had felt for many months, he closed the door of his cabin and buried his face in his hands.

Poor Hubert! His heart was growing as tender as it was once hard, and recent sickness had unfitted him to encounter, without emotion, the many visions of that youth-time which now came so vividly before him.

"God grant that I may find them living," he said earnestly, but then his memory brought back again some of the forebodings and inward whisperings which had often, in bygone years, checked for a moment his reckless course, and his heart told him again that his mother was no more. It came like a deep sorrow to Hubert, like a mighty wave throwing back every torrent upon which it rolled, but he had learned how to contend with grief and soon the dim cabin lamp was lighted and as night grew dark, he sat and read the much-treasured portion of his mother's Bible. He gained comfort as he read page after page, and it may have been that the lamp grew brighter, at any rate, Hubert's face wore a happier beam and when the sailor came into the cabin, he said, "Good evening, your honour; glad to see your honour looking better and cheerful like."

"Better, Ben! Have I looked ill today?"

"Not ill, exactly, your honour," said Ben, "but a little landsman like, just about the time the passengers for Portugal got adrift; when Mr. Collinton, your honour's friend, left."

The Wanderer's Return

"Well, Ben, I was sorry to lose him, but how late it is! Why, I have been reading two hours!"

With the assistance of the sailor, Hubert retired to rest, but, just as Ben was leaving the cabin, Hubert requested that he would reach him the Bible that lay upon the table.

"I have a better Bible than this, your honour," said Ben, as he handed the book, "I mean one that has it all in, not torn as this is, and, if your honour likes, I'll fetch it, though it's not to every one I'd lend it."

"Why do you offer to lend it to me, then?"

"Because, your honour, I'm sure you think a great deal of the Bible, and it's a pity you haven't one with all in, this has been bad enough used at any rate, but some folks don't care how they destroy the Bible. I'm glad it's got into your honour's hands, but if you'll accept the loan of mine, I shall be proud to lend it to you, there's not a leaf out; it was the last thing my poor mother ever gave me, and I have used it now over twenty years."

"Thank you, Ben, I do not wish it, mine is torn, I know, but it will do for me. Thank you all the same. Good night."

Hubert was glad when he found himself alone, he was in the habit of talking with Ben, but the sailor's homely remarks were not quite agreeable to him now. Poor untaught fellow, how nobly he appeared to rise in that night's shadows, children of penury, perhaps, he and his mother, yet how rich in affection! Hubert thought many times of that sailor's Bible; like his own, it was a mother's gift, but it had *all* in, while his had been ruthlessly destroyed. Memory brought back many a long forgotten scene,

The Wanderer's Return

when his hard heart strove to rise against the silent admonitions which the sight of that book was ever wont to give, and as he grasped all that was left to him now, a deep and heartfelt prayer from his penitent heart ascended to the throne of God.

The vessel in which Hubert sailed had made a quick run to England, and in a few days after the passengers left for Portugal, Hubert landed upon the shores of his native country, and never before had he felt so lonely. He was home without a home, however, being still under orders from the East India Company, he referred to his papers, and then immediately proceeded to London. Lame, without friends, and amongst strangers, Hubert longed to be making his way to his own native village, but he was compelled to tarry some time in London; at length, however, he received his discharge with a handsome pension, and was at liberty to go where he pleased.

Now Hubert felt undecided; he scarcely knew what to do. At one time he thought of writing home and telling them he was coming, but to whom could he write? Then he thought of taking the coach at once home, but another thought made him abandon that, for his heart was not yet schooled to the task of facing those he had so cruelly injured.

Hesitating what to do, another week passed by, and his conscience, at length, so smote him for lingering, that after arranging about his luggage, which was still at the Custom-house, and which he preferred should for the present remain there, he set out with one small trunk, and commenced his journey northward. So many years had passed since Hubert had come along the road by which he was returning, that he might have been in a foreign land: he remembered nothing, but he thought the country beautiful, and when evening came on, he alighted

The Wanderer's Return

from the coach, and stayed for the night at a small town. The journey had been rather too much for him: still he felt anxious to be getting on; so, when the coach passed through the town on the following day, he proceeded some distance further. Four days had passed; Hubert, by short stages, was drawing near his home, and the nearer he came to it, the more anxious and nervous grew his heart; he would have given much to have known which of his family remained. Once, years ago, while in a frenzied mood, when rage and passion overcame him, he was suddenly called back to reason by a mystic shadow crossing his vision: it may have been that a heated brain brought before his fierce eye that which startled him, but the remembrance of that moment had seldom left him, and he felt certain that his mother, at least, was missing in his father's household.

Another short journey had been made, and a candle was placed upon the parlour table in the little village inn, where Hubert, tired and wary, intended staying for the night. Many of the villagers had seen him leave the coach at the inn door; he was wrapped in a blue cloak, and walked lame, resting upon a stick, his bearing perhaps, or it may have been a whisper, told them that he was a soldier, and there was a fair chance of a good evening for the landlord of the King George.

One by one the parlour received its guests, and more candles were brought in; a log too - for it was the month of October - found its way to the fire, and the landlord told his wife to see to the customers, for he was going to join the company in the parlour.

Hubert saw with some uneasiness the people coming in, and he would gladly have retired to rest, but his coming was an event they were unwilling to let pass unobserved, and they gathered

The Wanderer's Return

round him with so much kindness and sympathy, that Hubert felt constrained to stay with them.

The old armchair in he corner, which was sacred to two purposes - namely, once a year, when they had beaten the bounds, the vicar sat in it in the tent, to partake of the roast beef, which was bountifully provided for those good old observers of ancient customs, and once a year, when the village club was held, the lord of the manor occupied it again. Duly polished every week was that dark oak chair, and not even the sage-looking cat attempted to usurp it. This evening, that honoured seat was drawn up to the fire, a large cushion was placed in it, and there the tired soldier rested.

They saw he was lame, and one went and fetched a soft stool for his wounded leg; then as they sat around him, with their honest sympathetic hearts beating warmly towards the brave defenders of their country, what could Hubert do but tell them of the battles won, and many incidents that make up the soldier's life in India? He had much to tell, and they listened eagerly to him till the hour grew late, and Hubert felt that a soldier's heart still beat in his bosom, and the fire of his youth had not died out. They felt it too, but their enthusiasm was tempered by the constant reference that Hubert made to the God who had preserved him. They parted for the night as the village clock struck eleven, and many of them wondered, as they walked homeward, where he was going, and why he was traveling alone - questions they had not yet ventured to ask, but they promised each other before they parted that they would come again to the inn on the morrow.

CHAPTER XI

HOME AT LAST

My father's house once more, in its own moonlight beauty! Yet around something amidst the dewy calm profound broods, never mar'd before.

* * * *

My soul grows faint with fear, even as if angel steps had mark'd the sod; I tremble when I move - the voice of God is in the foliage here.

Hubert was not much refreshed when the morrow came, the weather had changed during the night, and the rain fell heavily, and his wounded leg was so painful that he determined upon not proceeding on his journey, but requested permission to walk in the well-kept secluded garden at the back of the house, if the rain cleared off.

It was a dreary morning, but about noon the sun shone out, and Hubert, leaning upon his staff, bent his steps to the snug little summerhouse in the garden. It was a quiet spot, and Hubert was glad to be there alone. The storm was over, the few remaining autumn flowers were fading, and the leaves were falling thickly from the trees, and Hubert, as he looked upon the scene around him, drew a deep sigh, and taking from his pocket his "torn Bible," began to read.

Absorbed in what he was doing, he did not see a little boy approach the summerhouse, and it was not until a small spade fell accidentally from the child's hand that he noticed him.

Home at Last

"Ah! Do you live here?" inquired Hubert.

"No, sir, but grandfather does, and he told me you were here."

"Did he send you to me?"

"No, sir, but he told me you had fought a great many battles, and I wanted to see you because I am going to be a soldier - when I'm a man, I mean."

"How old are you now?"

"I'm eight, sir, but you know, I shall be older soon, and perhaps as big as you are."

"Perhaps so," said Hubert, with a smile; "and what's your name?"

"Frank, sir - Frank Lyons - the same as father's and grandfather's, but they are not soldiers, you know. I am going to be a soldier," and then, fixing his eyes upon a medal which Hubert wore upon his breast, he eagerly asked all about it. Hubert was amused at the little fellow, and answered many an inquiry he made, and as he was listening to something Hubert was saying, all at once he caught sight of the "torn Bible," and taking it in his hand, he said -

"Is this a Bible, sir? Oh, how it's torn! Did it get torn like this in the battles?"

"No, child, but," pointing to the hole in the cover, "it got that in the last battle I was in."

Home at Last

Frank looked for some time at the hole the bullet had made; then looking up into Hubert's face, he said, thoughtfully –

Sir, don't you think God was very good to take care of you in the battles?"

"He was, child; He has always been good to me."

"Then why did you let any one be so wicked as to tear this Bible so?"

Hubert kissed the boy's cheek: he could not answer the home thrust, but taking the Bible from his hand, said –

"Good-bye, Frank, now run away home."

The child went away as he was desired, but Hubert's heart reproached him in a moment; he thought he had been harsh, so, bending forward, he called the little fellow back.

There was a tear in the boy's eye when he returned, and stood gazing up again into Hubert's face, which convinced Hubert that he had disappointed him, so taking his little hand, he said-

"Frank, do you wish to ask my anything more?"

Home at Last

Hubert and the Child

Home at Last

"Yes, sir, I want to ask all about being a soldier."

Hubert could not resist, nor refuse to listen to the inquiries of that little heart. And there they sat - the once disobedient, sinning, reckless son, and the little artless child. It relieved the older bosom to talk of the past, and Hubert told into that little ear more than he had told any one before. It was a strange sympathy, but the boy drew closer to him, leant his little arms upon the veteran's knee as he gazed earnestly into his face, while Hubert told him something of his own youth-time, and about being a soldier.

"Then you have been a soldier longer than I've been born," said Frank. "How glad your mother will be to see you! I think I should run all the way; I would not stop at all till I got home."

"But could you run, Frank, if you were as lame as I am?"

"No, sir, I could not, but then I would ride - I would never stop anywhere until I got home."

"But if you were in pain what would you do?"

"Oh, I would not mind it at all; soldiers ought never to mind pain. When Charley wheeled the big barrow over my feet I did not cry, though he hurt me dreadfully, because I am going to be a soldier. But that is grandfather calling me. Goodbye, sir!"

In an instant the boy was gone, and Hubert, bending forward, looked out along the side pathway down which he had run. He watched him until he was out of sight, and then his thoughts turned upon himself. Why was he contented in tarrying there?

Home at Last

How was it that he felt no spirit to hurry onward? He looked up at the sky, the clouds were breaking, and the sun shone brightly.

"Oh, that I were at home," he uttered, "and all the past forgiven! How can I face it?" But no good thought came into his mind to help him in his difficulty, and he sat for some time gazing vacantly into the garden.

"Yes, little Frank," he suddenly exclaimed, "they will be glad to see me; I'll not stay here." And taking his stick in his hand, he drew his cloak around him, and went into the house. The good people were somewhat unwilling to part with their visitor, but Hubert was determined to go, and as he parted with the kind people, they were astonished to see him kiss little Frank, and then to hear him say -

"Goodbye, Frank. I'm not going to stop any more till I get home. Learn to read your Bible, and I hope you will make a good soldier."

The old landlord felt honoured at the notice Hubert had taken of his grandson, and as he removed his own little old black hat from his head, he turned to the child, and said -

"Your bow, Franky; make a bow to his honour - it may be he's a general."

General or not, it mattered but little to Frank, for, taking Hubert's hand, he said -

"Goodbye, sir; I *will* try and be a good soldier."

Home at Last

Many little incidents, besides the one here recorded, befell Hubert as he journeyed homeward, and though he was long upon the way, he might have been longer, had not little Frank's words - "How glad your mother will be to see you!" - so rung in his ears, that he felt compelled to go on, and the next afternoon to that on which he left the village inn, his heart began to beat as he thought he recognized some old places. Ah, yes! There was the old white tollgate - he knew it was just one mile from his home; so here he alighted from the coach, and leaving his luggage with the man who kept the gate, he walked gently on his way.

The day was closing, the labourers were returning from the field, and Hubert looked earnestly into the face of many he met, to see if he could recognize any of them. He did not in his heart quite wish to be known, but the incentive to find some friend of other years was powerful, and there was a slight hope for a familiar face; he, however, met no one that he knew, so he turned aside into a shady lane. Hubert knew the place well; often in his boyish days that lane had been his play place - it was his favorite haunt - and there now he sat down upon the same old grey stone, round, which so many memories of the past still hovered. From that large stone seat nearly every house in the village could be seen, and there in the valley it lay, in all the same calm beauty in which it had often risen before his view as he lay down beneath the sultry skies of India; there, too, was the cottage, with its white walls, over which the ivy still roamed at will - the same garden, not a path or tree seemed changed; there was the same white-painted gate, near which his family stood when he said the last goodbye to them; everything, indeed, looked the same - there appeared no change, save that which his heart led him to expect, and his coat felt tighter than usual across his chest, as he looked down from the hill upon his early home. He knew the way well -

Home at Last

he saw the narrow pathway that would lead him out against the gate of his father's house, and yet he had not courage to go there.

Night drew on, and still Hubert sat upon the stone, many persons passed him, and more than one gazed earnestly at him, for his dress was not familiar to them, and he heard them whisper as they passed, "who is he?" A few, more curious than the others, returned to take another look at him, but he was gone. "I am a coward," he had whispered to himself, and in the closing shadow of the night, had trodden the narrow pathway, and reached the white gate of his home. The walk down the hillside had wearied him, and he stayed a moment to rest upon his staff before he entered. He may have stayed longer than he intended, for an aged man, leaning also upon a staff, startled him by saying -

"You appear tired, sir; pray, have you far to go?"

"Not far; I hope to lodge in the village tonight. Does Mrs. Bird keep the White Swan now?"

"Mrs. Bird? Nay, she's in yonder churchyard; it's many a year since she died. You may have been here before, but it must be long since."

"Very long," said Hubert, with a sigh. "It is more than twenty years. Since then I have been fighting in the wars in India. Sir, I am a soldier."

"A soldier!" said the old man. "Ah, and from India - come in and rest a bit! From India, did you say? I once had a son there - come in, talk with me, if only for an hour. It may be that I may hear something of my boy. He went away nearly twenty-four years ago, and I never heard from him afterwards. Sometimes I

Home at Last

think he is dead, and then sometimes I don't. The neighbours feel sure he is dead, but sometimes I have an idea that I shall yet hear from him - I scarcely dare to hope it, though. Come, soldier, don't stand here, the evening is cold, walk up to the house, my little Richard will know where you can lodge for the night. He knows every one in the village."

Without uttering a single word, Hubert followed the old man. Richard saw them coming, and at his grandfather's bidding, drew another chair to the fire for the stranger.

The old man changed his shoes, and then, putting his feet upon a stool before the fire, turned his face to Hubert, as he said -

"There was a time when the very name of a soldier was hateful to me, but circumstances change one. I had a care for all my lads, but for that one that went into the army I had the most care, and it was better, perhaps, that he should be taken from me. For more than twenty years, though, I refused to be comforted for his loss, but I now do feel that it was God's will, for that boy was our eldest, and we thought a deal too much of him until he rebelled against us. He often stood between us and our Maker - I mean he had our first and best thoughts. It will not do, soldier, for the heart to worship more than one, and that one must be God. Our poor lad, God forgive him, paid us ill for our care - he was ungrateful - he forgot us! Bitterly, indeed, we felt the truth of the proverb, that, 'sharper than a serpent's tooth is an unthankful child.'" And the old man brushed away a tear; then, looking into the stranger's face, he added, "did you ever hear of a Hubert Goodwin in India?"

"Hubert Goodwin?" repeated Hubert, with a husky voice. "Goodwin? - but why should you think your son is dead, or

Home at Last

something may have prevented him. His letters may have been lost, or a thousand things happened, and he may have regretted the silence as much as you have."

"Is it possible," replied the old man, much excited, "that my poor lad ever thought I had forgotten him?" and he bowed his whitened head.

Before this little scene was half finished, the unworthiness of the part he was playing smote Hubert's heart, he had never intended offering any excuse for his past misconduct, and he felt so self-convicted at the sight of the grief he had so unwittingly caused, that, raising up the old man's head, he said, with deep emotion, "No, father; father, I had forgotten - not you."

"What, Hubert!" cried the old man, pushing him back, and wildly gazing at him. "Hubert! My Hubert! No!" Then he laughed, and then, pointing upward, he added: "perhaps he's up in heaven with the others, poor lad. I'll tell him there that I never forgot him: poor lad, he'll forgive me, I never forgot him."

While the old man was speaking, young Richard whispered something to Hubert, who immediately moved behind his father's high-backed chair.

"Grandfather, dear," said the boy, as he kissed his cheek, "why do you cry?"

"I don't know, boy. Oh, yes, just some thoughts of your uncle Hubert! But - " and he stared about, "where is the soldier, where is he, Richard? Was I dreaming? Was it Hubert? - Has he returned? - Where, where is he? Fetch him, Richard."

Home at Last

"I'm here, father;" and Hubert, as well as he was able, knelt before the old man.

"Oh, Hubert!" were the only words that were uttered, for the recognition in one moment was complete; long, very long, the old man wept upon the bosom of his son, and Hubert wept too; young Richard cried, perhaps because his dear old grandfather did, but Martha, the faithful servant of forty years, knew all the sorrows of her good old master - knew, too, all about the wandering sheep that had come home. She remembered when he was a little lamb in the fold, and she mingled the overflowing of her heart with the others; then she went and closed all the casement shutters, for they wished to have the joy of that first meeting to themselves. The prodigal had indeed returned, but friends and neighbours must not come and make merry yet - the fatted calf must not be killed till tomorrow.

No one intruded upon the scenes of Hubert's home on the evening of his return. The joy of once again seeing him - the answer to so many prayers - came as a new link in the chain of the old man's existence; he would have no supplication, no confession from his erring son: it was enough that the wanderer had returned, and it was *more* than enough, it was a joy that he had often prayed for, though his hope of knowing it had long since died, that Hubert might become a child of God. Poor old man! How tenderly and lovingly he strained his long-lost son to his bosom, and the most severe reproofs, denied forgiveness, or the bitterest reproaches, would not have been so hard for Hubert to endure as the tender affection of his deeply injured father.

Home at Last

Hubert's Return

Home at Last

Night closed around and the old man sat later by the fireside than he had done for years: for much of life's vigour had returned with his hopes and joy; he breathed the evening prayers with a deeper fervour; he joined in the evening hymn with a voice less tremulous than the others, and he walked without his staff to his bed.

Poor bereaved heart! Nearly all had been taken from him; none save the little orphan grandson had been left for him to love; the waters of affliction had rolled deeply over his head, but the heart, consecrated to heaven, had learnt to bow meekly to the rod, and now the most bitter cup of his life had been filled with joy. "Thy will be done," was the old man's closing prayer, as he lay down upon his pillow that night, and there was a holy calmness upon his brow, for peace and gratitude filled his heart.

Different, indeed, were the feelings Hubert endured, and as he shut himself in his bedroom - the bedroom of his boyhood - there was a deep struggle in his heart. More vividly than ever came the sins of his past life before him, and great indeed was the remorse he felt for the long years of woe he had caused. How he longed to tell all his repentance to his father! But the old man had forgiven him without; it would not, however, wipe away the sin he had committed, and the remembrance was like an inward fire - burning and burning continually. There was one, however, who *would* listen to his woe, and Hubert, on bended knee, poured it out from his swelling heart, no eloquence, no effort was needed, and as the hours of the night of deep repentance passed on, Hubert drew nearer and nearer to his Father in heaven, and the chastened heart became lightened; then he sunk to sleep as calmly as his father had done.

CHAPTER XII

MEMORIES OF CHILDISH DAYS

I stand on the brink of a river, the river of life to me, where the billows of memory quiver, and rise and fall like the sea.

I read in their tremulous motion the records of many a year, and like voices that come from the ocean are the muffled words I hear. - ANON

A bright morning beamed upon Hubert as he awoke from his slumber in his childhood's home; he looked round the room; somehow there were many things in it that he could recollect. There was the dark oak chest, with curious figures carved upon the front, which had often been a source of terror to him in early years because, on one occasion, he was told that they were the likenesses of certain naughty boys, whose remains he verily believed were within that black chest, and though for many years he had forgotten all about it, the story, and the nurse who told it, came all back fresh into his memory. Then there was the old-fashioned furniture upon the bed. "Why!" and he looked at it again, "it is the same, the very same, that covered me when last I slept here." And that large armchair behind the door, he knew *that*; he remembered that it was taken up there when he went to bed. Many other things there were that he remembered; very little, indeed, seemed changed, and as he looked round, his eyes lighted upon a stick, a bow, and a kite, tied together, hanging on the wall. He arose from his bed, and began to dress himself, scanning as he did so the various objects in his room. Presently he saw a small picture over the mantelshelf, and went to look at it. He started back, it was intended for himself; whether it had

Memories of Childish Days

been a good likeness he was not able to judge, but it represented him as a young soldier just going from home, and beneath it was written, "Our Hubert." It had been drawn from memory, and placed there in remembrance of the lost one; beneath it on the mantelshelf was a little box, and Hubert raised the lid - something more! Yes, something more; in that box lay a pair of slippers; they were little ones - a child of eight years old might have worn them - and Hubert, as he was just closing the lid, saw written inside it - "Our Hubert's." "Mine! Mine!" he said as he took them out; "not mine," but then some flash of memory lighted up the past, and he thought he could remember when they were his. Over these little slippers the soldier sat down and wept, for the truth had suddenly come to him, and he pictured his parents, gathering up every little thing that he had owned, remembering all about him, except that he had gone away and forgotten them, placing from the heart upon canvas the features of the rebellious one, and loving him fondly to the last. Perhaps over these little slippers they had shed many a tear; since they had covered the little feet, those feet had gone astray; what a dear relic they were of the past! How they reminded him of a time when he was pure and innocent! And he said, as he brushed away the tears from his cheeks -

"Oh! If I had only died then, I should have caused no sorrow, nor felt any, but been in heaven with the angels."

"Yes, Hubert, you would have caused sorrow," some spirit near him might have whispered; "firstborn of that dwelling, they could not spare thee. He who gave thee as a blessing at the first, means thee to be a blessing still."

Hubert replaced the slippers, and went downstairs to meet his father.

Memories of Childish Days

The old man was there first, years had passed since he had risen so early, but new life seemed to have been given to him, and as he met his long lost son at the door, he forgot that he was no longer the little child of his love; he forgot, too, all the sorrow he had been to him; forgot the long years he had mourned him, and clasped him fondly to his heart.

"Hubert," said his father, "it is thirty-nine years* this very day since I received you, my first-born child; a second time you have been born to me, and we shall do well to rejoice, your mother, dear sainted one, I would that she were here with us, but we will not wish her back - she is happier in heaven, and we will not sorrow because she's gone, it would seem like reproaching the good God, who, in his mercy, has restored you to me. Yes, boy, I know well that she bitterly wept your loss - your absence, I mean, but she wept the death of other dear ones, and God took her to them; we shall, I hope, join them soon. Heaven bless you!"

It was a happy day, sanctified by a holy joy. Many friends, including the good minister of the parish, who, thirty-nine years before, received Hubert at the font, and prayed to Heaven to bless him, brought their mead of welcome to the wanderer, and that faithful servant of his heavenly Master spoke comfort to his aged fellow-pilgrim's heart.

"Master Goodwin," he said, "I told you, years ago, that if ye pray and do indeed believe, that ye shall receive; it shall be as ye ask; it is the prayer without faith that wins no blessing. God does not give us all we ask, because we are sinning creatures, and know not what we ask, but then, how many of us pray for things that we never want! And if we had only ourselves to judge what is best for us, instead of receiving a blessing, we should often receive a

111

curse. When the heart asks God to teach it to pray, and then asks a blessing, believing that if it is God's will that prayer will be granted, depend upon that, that prayer is answered; if the actual thing is not given, the heart receives something in another way; at any rate, it *does* get a blessing. How many years you have prayed for that son, and how many times you murmured, and thought God had forgotten, but He never forgets, He has remembered all your grief, and answered, what prayer? Why, the prayer of faith. If you look back you will find that it is only of late years that you have borne your sorrows without murmuring; they have been heavy, we know; yet, for how many years the gilding of your prayers was tarnished by the breath of sorrowful repining, and perhaps, it was when your heart could really say, 'Thy will be done,' that the cloud of your troubles began to disperse, and the blessing was given. Oh, that men would always praise the Lord for his goodness! How well He knows all our need; He knows when to smite and when to heal, and they who continue faithful unto death, to them shall that mysterious providence be more fully revealed. If much sorrow has been your portion, so has much blessing. It is better to have saints in heaven than rebellious children on earth, and God has been very gracious to you."

"He has, indeed," said Hubert's father. "I feel it more truly now," and as he grasped the faithful pastor's hand, he said - "He gave you to this parish as one of my blessings, and your prayers have perhaps helped to restore me my son. Pray with us now, for our joy may be too great."

They knelt: a deep and earnest prayer fell from the pastor's lips upon the stillness of the hour, and the tear upon the cheek told its power on the heart. The prayer was over, and the good man, bidding them adieu for the present, left them to rejoice over the

Memories of Childish Days

once lost one, while he, in the spirit of his mission, withdrew himself from the world, and thanked God for having brought back the wandering sheep.

Hubert's return had filled his father with such joy that he would scarcely tell him anything about the family, so anxious was he to hear all about himself, and it was some time after his arrival before he heard of all the bereavement of that household. All gone! - All whom he had left in the beauty and strength of youth, when he went out to India, had been swept to the tomb; not one left round that desolate hearth, except the little orphan Richard, now nine years old, the only child of his second brother, who, with his young wife, had sunk into an early grave. One by one the hand of death had taken them from the fireside, and it was now his turn to mourn them. He saw plainly now how it was that his father had received him so fondly. Poor old man! His home had been sadly lonely; the household gods had been all broken, and his aged heart nearly so. Hubert looked at his father as he told the history of each one as they had departed, and conscience told him that there was before him a braver warrior than he had ever seen before; one who had fought a stern battle, and had ever been in the thickest of the fight. Hubert's heart beat; he felt that he had added heavily to the burden and heat of his father's day, and falling upon his knee before his parent, he cried, as his hands covered his face - "oh, father, forgive me!"

"Forgive you! Oh, Hubert, did I forget to say I had forgiven you long ago? There is nothing now to forgive, but I bless you for coming home. Let the past be the past. Bless you for coming home to me! God is good, he gave, he has a right to take, but he has given you to me again." But the truth seemed to shine upon the old man's mind, and putting his arm round Hubert's neck, he said -

Memories of Childish Days

"Ah! Well, it's all forgiven; you might have done other than you have done, perhaps, but never mind," and he wept tears of joy upon the bosom of his son. This little rebuke from Hubert's father was more welcome than the caresses he received, and Hubert opened his heart upon it, and began to tell his father of things which had befallen him in India, hitherto he had seldom spoken, except in answer to his father's many questions, for there was a weight of remorse in his bosom, which nothing yet had removed, but now he was assured of his father's forgiveness, and a smile lighted up his hitherto sad face, as they sat round the fire telling many a story of his distant home; his father was delighted, and young Richard drew his little chair beside his veteran uncle, to listen also. Many a week passed by; Hubert had ever something to tell his father, but of all the history of the past, or of all the fame he had won, nothing was so dear to the old man's heart as the "Torn Bible;" he made Hubert tell again and again all about it, its long neglect, and its abuse. The field of battle, the capture, and the rescue from the Indians, and even the dreadful night in the jungle, when Hubert's lifeblood was draining from his wounds, were nothing compared with the strong will broken, the heart subdued, and the torn, despised Bible giving back a new and better life to the prodigal. Oh, how the old man loved to dwell upon that! Many prayers from the long since silent heart had been answered then, and he ever repeated in Hubert's ear the words, "oh, yes, she knew all about it, for she was in heaven and rejoiced when you repented."**

Hubert grew happier in the society of his father, and though at times a kind of reflection on his past life would cast a sort of thoughtful sadness over his brow, yet his health daily improved, and his heart became more and more attuned to the will of God.

Memories of Childish Days

* There is a discrepancy of two years between Hubert's account of his age and his father's account of Hubert's age. This difference does not change or affect the theme of this story.

** Original text: "oh yes, she knew all about it, for she was one of the angels in heaven that rejoiced when you repented."

CHAPTER XIII

AT REST

Gales from heaven, if so he will, sweeter melodies can wake, on the lonely mountain rill, than the meeting waters make who hath the Father and the Son, may be left, but not alone. - KEBLE

Years rolled away. Hubert's history in the village became almost a thing of the past; the young, who had paid a sort of homage to him, for his warrior fame, had almost forgotten it, and had grown up to reverence him for his goodness, and the aged, as he sat by many a dying bed, blessed him with their latest breath. Ever, day by day, did Hubert take his staff and go forth to comfort some less favoured brother, and the "Torn Bible" - guide of his present life - accusing, yet dear relic of his past, soothed many a departing spirit, and helped to ripen his own for Eternity.

Since Hubert's reunion with his father, he had found many new friends, but he did not forget his old ones: to those in India he occasionally wrote, and occasionally received letters; still, it was a source of great regret to him that he did not hear anything of the companion of his voyage with whom he parted off Lisbon. While the first year after his return home was passing, he scarcely thought anything of not hearing from him, but the second year, and third, and now the fifth had come, without tidings of his friend, and with a pang of deep and silent regret, he began to conclude that he had died, though notwithstanding this thought, there was a lingering hope that his friend would yet come, and it was sometimes when his heart felt sad, that the wish for his friend became strong, perhaps upon the wish grew the hope, and

At Rest

then Hubert would take his staff and wander up the hill-side, out to the little white tollgate, and then walk a mile or two down the broad road that led to the south. There was a rude seat by the roadside, formed of gnarled and moss-grown branches, intermixed with stones: beside it was a huge stone trough, which a kindly mountain stream kept ever filled with water; over it, shading it from the sun, branched a stately oak, and this spot was a resting place for man and beast. Hubert often walked there, sat down and rested beneath the tree, and looked with longing eyes down the road; still his friend came not, and he as often returned sadder than he went. How little he thought that his father had trodden that same road with a heavy heart for many a year, in the fond hope of meeting him, though there was but little probability in either instance that the hope would be realized; one moment's reflection would have told the heart so, but the heart under such circumstances seems unwilling to reflect - or even if it does, the effect is transitory, and the heart hopes on again against hope, and it is a blessed thing, this hope - for how often in the dark hour it throws a ray of light upon the darkness that is felt, and keeps a soul from despair.

Hubert had been six years at home, and for many months had not been along the road where he was wont to go; indeed, he had sighed over the memory of his friend, and at last had ceased to expect him, but now an unexpected joy had befallen him, for Mr. Collinton was coming. Hubert was delighted, and he read the letter many times over; his father was delighted too, for Hubert had confided to that parent, whom he now so loved and honoured, all his secret about the stranger, and the old man partook of the longing to see the friend, a portion of whose life had been so strangely linked with that of his son.

At Rest

Hubert had often wondered how it was that the letter, which he had written to his friend, telling him of his safe arrival at home, had not been answered, but it appeared that that letter had been duly received, and that Mr. Collinton, acting upon its contents, was now, after a long delay, making his way to Hulney.

One morning, after rising somewhat earlier than usual, Hubert took his staff, went up the hillside, and took his way towards the seat by the roadside; it was still early, yet Hubert appeared to be in haste; he passed the white tollgate, wished good morning to the man who kept it, and stayed a moment to inquire what time the coach would pass by, and then he went on his way again until he came to the seat by the roadside, where he sat down and looked with an anxious eye for the coach coming. Mr. Collinton had not told him the exact day that he would come, but this was the last day of the week, and Hubert felt sure that it would bring him, and he was not wrong. The coach, with its living burden, came at last, and Hubert and his friend met again. "Leave the luggage at my house," said Hubert to the coachman, whom he now well knew, and then he and his friend sat down beneath the shady tree. How glad they were to meet again! And then Hubert soon told him that he was none other than the soldier lad who in years gone by had won his heart. The stranger listened with astonishment; gazed at him with a deeper earnestness than ever, and tears rushed to his eyes as he grasped his hands. And why did he feel so? There was nothing now in the face of that war-worn soldier which reminded him of the dear one he had buried; nothing now to make him feel, as he once said he had felt, that some of his love for the dead seemed to centre in him, and yet he did love him, and it was to find him again that he had given up the world, and taken his way to that little northern village, for he had felt, ever since he had parted with Hubert off Lisbon, all the emptiness of life without pure religion. He had felt a void in his heart that nothing around him could fill, and though he tarried longer upon the continent than he had intended, he ever thought of Hubert, and as he told him, as they sat together by the roadside, it was his memory and the hope of seeing him again that had blessed his life, and made him long to join him, that they might read and study God's Word.

"Why have you been so long in coming?" asked Hubert. "I thought, at most, your absence would be but one year, but when it was two, then three, and now nearly six, I gave you up."

"And thought me dead, perhaps?"

"Yes, sometimes I thought it might be so, for I could not think you had forgotten."

"No, no, you are right there; I never could forget: but traveling in Portugal and Spain, those countries full of such deep interest, I know I tarried, but when I was uneasy here in my heart, and my thought would turn nowhere but to you, I prepared to make my way to you. Sometimes, an opportunity lost threw off my plans; sometimes, the desponding mood I had fallen into was suddenly dispersed by some event: and so I wandered up and down, amongst the many beauties and enchantments of Spain - not forgetting you, my friend, but tempting Providence by deferring to come to you. Oh! It was a sin, and I felt it, but I hadn't you there, nor any one to say the words you might have said. And so I lingered, but I gave in at last. I was not happy there, and it has struck me many a time, that there is many a man in this world whose life has been a continuous fluctuation between right and wrong - knowing what was right, being anxious to do what was right, and yet ever doing wrong: how is it?"

At Rest

"My friend," said Hubert, putting his hand upon the stranger's knee, "the Bible says that the heart of man is inclined to do evil, and is it not so? Still, there is that in man which makes him love to do good - do right, I mean, and as far as I can judge, man generally makes an effort to do so. But here is the mistake: he too often has a false idea of what is right, and follows his own notions of right and wrong, rather than the standard laid down in God's Word. His inclination to do evil makes him too often try to make out that evil to be good, and so he goes on, spending a whole life in error, while all the time he fancies he is perfectly right. When a man's heart is not right with God, he must ever be going wrong, but somehow, we don't like to be told it - I know I did not. Think of the years I spent in India in all kinds of sin, and all the time I wished the world to think well of me, and tried to persuade myself that I was perfectly right. But what a life it was! How many things occurred to tell me that I was wrong! But I would not hear, and continued a wicked course, trying to please man, and caring nothing whatever about God. I was worse than the heathens."

"How? You had the Bible with you in India."

"I had," replied Hubert, "and therefore I was the more guilty and responsible for the life I led there. I cannot look upon man without the Bible as I do upon him with: it is the *only* source from which we can draw a perfect rule of life, and if man has it not, how can he know? Whether he reads it or not is another matter: if he has it at all he is responsible."

"Ah!" said the stranger, "I shall do now; we can talk these matters over together; somehow, I know all this, but yet I cannot get on with it alone. How is your father? Is he still living?"

At Rest

"Yes, and will be glad to see you; I have told him all we know of each other, and he is waiting now for our coming: for, like myself, he thought you would be here today."

As Hubert finished speaking, he and his friend rose from his seat, and walked to the village, and as they walked along Hubert told him of the devastation that death had caused in his home, and begged him, as he was the last of his family, to make his dwelling with them.

It was a goodly welcome that met the stranger at Hubert's home, and there was so much peace and happiness, sanctified by that religion which he longed for, that he soon became as one of the family, and by paying a yearly visit to the grave at Dunkeld, where he had buried his loved ones, he lived for ten years with Hubert and his father, and when he died, they mourned the loss of a Christian and a friend, and buried him as he had wished in the grave of his wife and son. Five years more were meted out to Hubert's father, and then they laid him with the dear ones gone before, and carved a simple record upon the stone that covered the grave where he and his wife lay.

"They sleep in Jesus," was all that Hubert told the world of them, and very soon the grass and flowers covered that fond testimony.

Between Hubert and Dr. Martin, in India, a warm friendship continued for many years; it ever cheered Hubert's heart to hear from his distant friend, for he owed him much, and heard from him gladly, but one day, after a longer silence than usual, there came a letter written by a stranger's hand, bearing the unwelcome news that the good man was gone. He had spent a long life of usefulness, and in the land, which had always been the field of his labour, he lay down and died. It was not his lot to hang up his

At Rest

weapons of warfare, and rest upon the laurels he had won, his Master was the King of kings, in whose cause he spent all his life. How could he rest? There was no reward on earth a sufficient recompense for his labours, and though his body now rests in an unknown distant tomb, yet, far away in the city of the great King, he has been crowned with an immortal diadem. How many quiet unobtrusive Christians there are, of whom the world knows nothing, who live to reclaim and guide aright their weak and sinning brethren, and though they live, and appear to die unknown, they give to many a dying bed peace, when there would be no peace, and they are often the ten-nay, the five - that save the city.

Hubert was sad at the news of his friend's death, but he knew where he should meet him again, and not as he felt when he remembered the young sinning companion of his youth, the never-forgotten Harris, with a grateful, thankful heart, he could think of him in heaven, and hope to meet him there.

Once more let us turn to Hubert's home. Young Richard, dear good boy, when he grew to manhood, married the playfellow of his childhood, the orphan granddaughter of the village pastor, and they lived in the old house with Hubert, and when, at last the veteran's career was ended, they followed him with many tears to the old churchyard, and Richard had that seventh white stone carved to his memory; it is but a simple unemblazoned record of one departed; yet travelers say it is a strange device, that torn, ill-used book, and ever and anon someone asks its meaning.

Our story is ended, and we would ask the reader to remember that Hubert's life is not a fiction. And shouldst thou ever wander to that old churchyard, sit down amidst its shadows, amongst its silent dead, perchance a fitful vision of thine own life may flit

At Rest

past thee - some whisper may re-echo a mother's prayer or a father's counsel and it may not be altogether unprofitable to thee to remember the history of Hubert and

THE TORN BIBLE.

Appendix

Key events and terms:

1777—Hubert was born.

1792— At the age of fifteen, Hubert leaves home for India.

1807— At the age of thirty-three, Hubert meets Ellen Buchan.

1811— At the age of thirty-seven, Hubert severely wounded by an ambush.

1811—Hubert returns to Hulney (Hulne Priory), England.

1847—Hubert dies and is buried in the old churchyard, he was seventy years old.

****

Beating the Bounds—an ancient custom in Britain and in Europe dating back over 2000 years and still practiced today. In essence, it involves local inhabitants of a church, walking their church property, farms, civic boundaries etc. and pausing as they pass certain trees, walls and hedges that denote the extent of the boundary to exclaim, pray and ritually beat particular landmarks with sticks. The ceremony might involve the blessing of crops or animals and the inspection of fences.

Captain—highest rank attained by Hubert.

Appendix

English East India Company—formally (1600-1708) Governor And Company Of Merchants Of London Trading Into The East Indies, or (1708-1873) United Company Of Merchants Of England Trading To The East Indies, English company formed for the exploitation of trade with East and Southeast Asia and India, incorporated by royal charter on Dec. 31, 1600. Starting as a monopolistic trading body, the company became involved in politics and acted as an agent of British imperialism in India from the early 18th century to the mid-19th century. In addition, the activities of the company in China in the 19th century served as a catalyst for the expansion of British influence there—Encyclopedia Britannica.

Flodden Field—a major border battle fought in the year 1513, between King James IV of Scotland and King Henry VIII of England. The Scot's king fell with the majority of the Scottish noblemen and hence, the end of Scotland as a separate country.

Hulney (Hulne Priory)—located north of Alnwick, England. Home village of Hubert Goodwin.

Margaret of Anjou—wife of King Henry VI, King of England. A great military leader who, with her forces, outflanked the Yorkists, under the Earl of Warwick, and defeated them at the second battle of St. Albans.

Religion—in this story, refers to a relationship with God through Jesus Christ.

ISBN 1553957814

Printed in Great Britain
by Amazon